Larry
A Novel of Church Recovery

By
Rev. Brian L. Boley

2nd Edition

ISBN 978-1-086876383
ODDPARTS PRESS
Oddparts.com

Introduction

Throughout North America, there are uncounted thousands of small churches that are struggling to survive and recover their vitality. Some are Baptist, some are Methodist, some are Presbyterian, some are Lutheran, some are Christian Churches, some are independent, some are rural Catholic congregations, and others belong to less common denominations. It is behind the pulpits of these small, struggling churches that new preachers are most likely to find themselves standing.

But there are few books that are designed to help the small church of less than 75 members – which is about the average size of a North American Protestant church. And leadership seminars are of little use – most consider any church with 200 active members to be a small church, yet we who lead them know that there is a tremendous difference in capability between a church of 150 members and a church of 25 members.

The denominational leaders are of little help, for their time is spent with the 500 and 2000 member churches. Why waste time on a twenty-person church when we have multiple Sunday school classes that are twice that size in many churches? And so the pastors and elders and deacons and lay leaders of the small churches are left to struggle and experiment, to try to adapt ideas intended for churches with many more resources to their churches, churches with a handful of truly active members and a couple of dozen elderly people who are not able to help much outside of Sunday morning.

Yet in these churches there are always a few committed people, people who are grieving because their church is dying, people who understand how important it was that their church stood in that particular location in times past, people who have memories of baptisms, of bible schools, of revivals, of great, wonderful, life-changing sermons – and people with memories of church fights, of poor pastors, of financial problems, of dull and boring days in those same pews.

It is to these loyal, grieving laypeople like yourself that this book is intended, a novel which can be read by a small weekly fellowship group. It is for you, the small church pastors who may be leading two, three, or even more churches and need ideas on how to grow small churches without a budget. It is for the committed but exhausted part-time pastor who works another full-time job in order that *this* particular church will not close. And it is for the new student pastor who is in his or her first church, trying to make all those seminary and bible college ideas work in the real world. It is hoped that many of these ideas will be helpful and useful and life-giving to your churches.

My wife and son and I have led small churches. Between us, we have led twenty-one churches, the largest of which has typical Sunday attendance of 115 people, and the smallest of which has had attendance of one to three people. I have attended churches in the Atlanta suburbs and on the West Virginia back roads. Church members ranged from doctors and lawyers, to schoolteachers and college professors, to goat farmers and truck drivers, to recovering drug addicts and people who had been retired for thirty years. The issues in the churches were always different – yet always the same.

Many of these ideas have come together as I prepared district- and state-level courses training lay leaders of churches. Other ideas simply arose as the Holy Spirit advised me how to proceed with problems in the churches I have pastored.

This book is the fictionalized story of a couple of churches and how their pastors, with special help, turned around the churches. This book uses the form and style of a novel to bring sound principles into the church, principles that work, principles that can lift a church from death's door to vitality and promise. This "teaching novel" style has a history of success in such books at *In His Steps* by Charles M Sheldon, *The Noticer* and *The Noticer Returns* by Andy Andrews, and, in a different realm, *The Goal* by Eliyahu Goldratt.

Questions are provided at the end of each chapter to encourage discussion. It should be noted that, while my theology is that of an evangelical Wesleyan, the vast majority of the concepts presented are applicable to almost any small church.

Additional information on the ideas presented in this book can be found in my sermon blog at brianboleysermons.blogspot.com.

Rev. Brian L. Boley

Quiet Dell, WV

June, 2018

Table of Contents

Additional Copies of this book may be ordered at:

Amazon.com

Lulu.com (bulk pricing available)

Or by calling 1-888-728-2465

Rev. Brian L. Boley is available for speaking and teaching events. To contact, call 1-888-728-2465 or visit oddparts.com

Other Books by Rev. Brian L. Boley include:

   What do Evangelical Christians Believe?

Prelude

"Pull over at the next exit and find a motel," the still, small voice said as the wind rocked the car. *"This is your next assignment."*

Larry put on his blinker and exited right. He'd been traveling for four hours, much of it in the rain. But the rain had stopped about an hour ago, just as he passed Columbus heading East on I-70. What time was it? 8:57 pm? *"Good,* "Larry thought, *"I can get a decent night's sleep."*

There, ahead of him was a cheap motel. He pulled in, took his bag out of the car, and was blown by a strong gust of wind into the lobby and began to speak with the young man behind the desk…

Chapter One - Lost in Her Grief

Shirley McDonald was sitting at her dining room table, reading the county paper, when she glanced at the "Fifty Years Ago" column. Among several items listed, it showed that her church had had a group baptism. Fifteen people were baptized that day. Shirley's name was listed.

She thought about her church and the hundred and fifty people that attended in those days. Last Sunday, Easter Sunday, there were only 31 people at the service – including the pastor.

All of a sudden, Shirley began to cry. She put down her head.

Through her life, from the days when she had been a young girl, Shirley had known that church. She started to attend the church when she was fourteen because a friend brought her. She had been baptized when she was fifteen. Five years later, she was married in that church. All five of her children were baptized in that church. Her two daughters were married in that church, and one son was married there. Her mother's funeral was held in the church two years ago. And through all those years, there were happy memories of bible studies and women's circles, of rummage sales and fellowship dinners, of wonderful sermons – and dull, boring sermons. And special times where the bread and grape juice – Shirley's church never used wine – had come together to make Christ alive in her.

And now it was clear that her church was dying.

The town was fine. It was stable – people said the last census had shown an increase of about 2 percent in the population. There were hundreds of young people at the football games, and the shops downtown bustled at Christmas and on summer afternoons. But the churches were dying. And something important was leaving Shirley's hometown, slowly, steadily. Year after year, attendance had been dropping at Shirley's church – and at others in town.

She had a vision of lying in a coffin and there not being enough men left in the church to carry her coffin out. So the undertaker and the pastor rolled her out and the doors closed and were padlocked. A black cat walked in front of the door and took up a position guarding it. The cat glared at her with an evil grin.

Shirley woke with a start. She must have fallen asleep!

She looked around sheepishly. Lying on the desk behind her was her Bible. She pulled it open. There, in front of her was Hebrews 5:11-12:

"We have much to say about this, but it is hard to explain because you are slow to learn. In fact, though by this time you ought to be teachers, you need someone to teach you the elementary truths of God's word all over again. You need milk, not solid food!"

Shirley looked up. Then she looked down. Was God sending her a message?

She began to pray aloud, and the tears flowed.

"Lord, help my understanding. My church is dying and I don't know why. I need you to send me a teacher, to send our pastor a teacher, to send our entire congregation a teacher who will tell us how to grow. We don't have much money, we don't have any young, strong bodies, but we have people who love you. Why are you letting us shrivel up and die? How have we failed you? Please forgive us and turn around our church."

Shirley continued her prayer, talking to the Lord about many things, but always coming back to her church and her desire that it would make a difference in her town. She finally stopped nearly 20 minutes later.

Eventually, she stood up, went to her phone and called an old friend of hers who lived in Atlanta. "Ruth, this is Shirley McDonald. I need your prayer help…"

When she hung up an hour later, she knew something good was going to happen. And over the next couple of months, she continued to pray for her church.

Discussion and Thought Questions

1)   What was your church like when you were young?

2)   How many people attended your church 30 years ago? 20 years ago? 10 years ago? 5 years ago? Last year?

3)   What is the trend?

4)   What are some of the possible reasons that your church attendance has the trend it has?

5)   Why is prayer a good first step in beginning any program?

6)   How long have you continued prayers for your church?

7)   What does the Prologue tell us about God's planning?

Chapter Two - The Pastor Meets a Stranger

Jerry Jones was almost in tears. He was a tall, good looking fellow with an easy smile and a good nature. Born and raised in the suburbs of Columbus, Ohio, Jerry found himself walking back to the parsonage of the Mount Carmel Church on a hot July morning with Shirley McDonald. Shirley had a tendency to stumble and since Jerry's parsonage was next door, he was the ideal strong arm for her to hold onto.

Jerry had been pastor at Mount Carmel for a year, and he was failing. His church had declined in attendance each year for the past fifteen years, and yesterday there were only twelve people who bothered to show up. Last summer, there were twenty. "Lord, what am I doing wrong? I need Your help!" Jerry quietly prayed as he walked quickly down the sidewalk after dropping Shirley at her door.

Jerry had his head down and didn't see the stranger sitting on the bench. So, when he tripped over the stranger's leg, Jerry hit the ground in a confused jumble of arms, legs, a Bible, and a yellow pad on which his sermon notes had been hurriedly written on Saturday night.

"Whoa, there. Are you ok?" the dark stranger said.

"I'll be fine…I guess," Jerry responded as he gathered together his things.

"You must be the pastor at the church down the lane," the stranger put it more as a statement than a question.

"Yes, sir," Jerry could now see that the stranger was older than himself, perhaps fifty or so, or maybe much older – it was hard to tell.

The stranger was lanky and lean, but only about five-foot-five. He had brown skin and features that indicated his ancestors had come from Turkey or Iraq or somewhere else in the Middle East. His hair was pure white and his brown eyes were piercing. He spoke with a perfect mid-west accent that sounded well-educated. And the hand that he offered Jerry was strong – very strong – but it appeared to be the hand of someone who had not done physical labor in many years. The man was wearing a plaid shirt and khaki pants that could have come from Wal-Mart - or Land's End.

"I hear that Mount Carmel is declining."

"Well…" Jerry started to deny the fact, but something in the stranger's eyes stopped him. "Yes, it looks like it will die in a year or so."

"That's a shame. You know, there are a lot of churches like yours. Fifty years ago, they were the center of their communities. Now, they're a social club for a few elderly people. That's not what the Lord intended."

Jerry perked up, "Are you a believer, sir?"

"Yes, I am. I have been for many years. By the way, you can stop calling me 'sir', and start calling me 'Larry'".

"Yes, sir…Larry. I'm Jerry Jones."

"Pleased to meet you, Pastor Jones."

They paused and considered each other for a moment. Larry continued, "You know, I led some churches for a while, years ago. Maybe I can give you some ideas that might help your church."

"I surely could use some help. Everything I've tried fails miserably."

"Well, sit down here, and let's talk."

Jerry sat down and began to spill out the story. This was his second posting. The first posting had been as a youth pastor at a big suburban church outside Dayton. Things had been great. Teens were excited and brought their friends to church. Many had been baptized and others were excited. And after three years in that position, the district supervisor had decided it was time for Jerry to have his own church.

Mount Carmel Church was located in a small village of a couple of thousand people, fifteen miles from the nearest Walmart. The church had an elderly congregation, with the youngest regulars being the Lockhart's, who were about 50 years old, and their grandson Ryan, who was thirteen. Most of the congregation were in their seventies but were in good health. Mable Johnson played the small organ sometimes, but more often preferred playing the piano because her knees hurt her these days. The congregation preferred to sing from a shaped note hymnal but would use the denomination's preferred hymnal if he insisted.

Jerry had tried having a series of outreach events. Although they had tried a pie sale, it had conflicted with the fireman's festival and only four people from outside the church had come. The church had offered a blood pressure screening and only one woman from outside the church had shown up. They had tried an "invite your friends to church" day. Three grandchildren showed up. And Christmas Eve, they had offered a living manger scene. About ten cars drove by, and Ethel Merrimac had caught pneumonia and nearly died.

"With all those events, not one adult came to our worship service, and even the grandchildren didn't come back," Jerry moaned. "I've read all the church growth books, but they don't seem to apply. They are all geared toward planting new churches or turning around big churches of a couple hundred people to grow them to become thousand-member churches. And their programs are too much for us. We simply don't have the people or the energy to start a Habitat for Humanity or send twenty people to clean up after a tornado. I'd love to start an inner-city mission, but the nearest inner city is fifty miles away! Nobody cares about fighting malaria, and I was the only person who showed up for the March against Breast Cancer, which was a bit uncomfortable. Our people don't have the money or the talents to do a big community passion play, and there's no need for a sports league – our people are lucky if they don't break a hip walking! There just don't seem to be any programs or missions that we can do!"

"Let me ask you something. What is the *mission* of your church?" Larry asked, leaning forward toward Jerry.

Jerry was silent for a few seconds. A dog barked in the distance a couple of times. "The mission?"

"Uh-huh."

"I guess I don't know."

Larry leaned back. "Jerry, I've been around a long time, and I've found that there are several things that can kill a church, but most churches die when they lose sight of their mission. Open up that Bible and look at Matthew 28, verses 18 through 20. Read that to me.

Jerry read, "*Then Jesus came to them and said, 'All authority in heaven and on earth has been given to me. Therefore, go and make disciples of all nations, baptizing them in the name of the Father and of the Son and of the Holy Spirit, and teaching them to obey everything I have commanded you. And surely, I am with you always, to the very end of the age.'*"

"*That* is the church's mission statement," Larry said. "Now, I want to take it apart for you. Is that okay with you?"

"Sure. It's Monday. I've got plenty of time," Jerry answered.

Jerry leaned forward again. "Okay. First, Jesus says He's been given 'all authority'. Do you believe this?"

"Of course," said Jerry. "That's what it means by 'Jesus is Lord'"

"That's right," Larry responded. "But that authority issue is critical. I've known a lot of people who say that 'Jesus is Lord', but don't really mean it. So once again, I ask you – do you believe that *all* authority in heaven and on earth has been given to Jesus Christ, including all authority over your entire life?"

Jerry started to answer quickly but stopped. He thought for a few minutes, thinking about what he wanted in life, and realizing that he really had often put other things in authority over Jesus in his life. "Larry, I guess you have me there. I've often thought that earning more money was more important than Jesus or pleasing the congregation was more important than Jesus. I guess I need to change that thinking."

"That is wisdom, and that will help you get a good start. I'm glad you're able to be honest with yourself – and with God," said Larry. He smiled a broad grin, and then he continued. "Many pastors today are confused and think that the Republican or Democratic Parties are the authority for what the church should do. Others think that the authority comes from their own feelings. It is critical that you realize that Jesus Christ is still living, and still has been given that authority."

"I do, but I guess I forget from time to time...well, *most* of the time...that I'm working for Jesus and not for anyone else," Jerry was contrite.

Larry was ready to move on. "Now, notice that the next thing Jesus says is 'Therefore'. If you believe that Jesus has been given all authority, 'therefore' you need to go and make disciples of all nations. He tells us to 'go' – we can't just hang around our house or the church building. We also have to make 'disciples of all nations.' Now, that means we need to think through a couple of steps.

"First, remember that Jesus was talking to His disciples. He was telling them to go and *make* disciples. *We* are those disciples. Someone made us into disciples. And now, we have to go make more people like ourselves.

"Second, a disciple is a student – and a follower. That means that if we are going to be disciples, we have to *study*, and we have to *follow*. We have to learn things and then practice them in real life. And remember that this applies to each member of your congregation, not just you, Pastor."

"I'll remember. But that's the hard part, isn't it?"

"Yes, of course it's the hard part. That why you're paid the big bucks – to help everyone in the congregation see that they need to become disciples, which is far more than just saying 'I believe in Jesus' and getting baptized. It means that *they* have become students and learn to follow Jesus and the Holy Spirit daily."

"But most of my people are saved and are satisfied with coming to church on Sunday mornings. In fact, some of them have told me they're not sure why Christians need to even bother coming to church after they've been saved."

"I'll get to that later and tell you how to change that. For now, accept that everyone is to become a disciple and let's see what this church mission is." Larry looked gentle, but there was an edge to his voice.

"Okay! I'll listen, "Jerry sat back to listen.

"Third, we are to make disciples of all nations – the original Greek word was *ethnui*, which is translated here as 'nations', and means "people groups". That means that we need to go to all people, not just people that look or sound like us. It means that we have to go to whites, blacks, Mexicans, Asians, rich, poor, middle class, working people, welfare people, married people, singles, widows, young people, kids, the mayor and the town drunk. In short, *all* means *all.*"

Jerry thought about his church, which was almost completely middle class.

Larry continued "...Furthermore, we have to baptize people and teach them to obey everything that Jesus commanded us – *including* this command to make disciples. So, we have to become disciples, *then* learn how to make disciples, *then* teach others how to become disciples *and* how to make disciples."

Jerry absorbed this for a moment. "I thought that the purpose of church was to worship God."

"It is," Larry responded. "You're partially right, there. But Jesus specifically wants that circle of worship to grow and expand. That won't happen unless existing disciples are intentional about making new disciples."

"I guess not." Jerry mulled over that thought in his mind. "Is there anything else I've missed?"

"Well, the other point is God's reason that He wants worship."

"What's that?"

"Let's get some lunch at Martha's hot dog stand, why don't we? My stomach is growling. I'll tell you on the way." Larry got up and began walking down the street. Jerry followed him.

After walking a minute or two, Jerry reminded his new friend, "You were going to tell me why God wants worship."

Larry stared hard at Jerry. "Truly learning to worship God changes people. You see, there are three types of people.

"The first type of people are arrogant and self-centered. They are so focused upon "success" that they can't achieve it, or they are so focused upon "happiness" that they can't be happy. The *real* problem is that these people are so focused upon themselves that they are their own god. They truly believe that they can handle anything, even assuming that when they die they'll figure out something or Someone will give them a life preserver. They have a hole in their heart, a missing piece called humbleness, an understanding that the Universe doesn't revolve around them.

"The second type of people are beaten-down and self-centered. They are so focused upon their problems that they feel they can't ever become happy or successful. They think that everything will turn out terrible, no matter what. The hole in their heart that they are missing is called self-respect, an understanding that they have value and worth simply because they are unique creatures of God. Deep down, they truly believe that they will die and that will be the end, or that the next life will be even worse than this one has been for them.

"The third type of person has been made whole by his or her encounter with God through Jesus Christ. Because they now have no fear of death, they have both self-respect and humbleness. The Holy Spirit has filled the holes in their hearts. Therefore, they are reasonably successful, reasonably happy, and reasonably nice. The best ones improve every day, becoming more and more holy. These are the people we call "disciples" of Jesus."

"So, to sum up, God has us worship to turn us into more pleasant people to be around?" Larry stopped and turned toward Jerry. "But why should He care about that?"

"Here's a way to think about it. Have you ever met a kindly old woman who always smiled?"

Jerry thought a second. There were a couple of these women in his church, like Shirley McDonald. "Yes."

"And have you ever met a cantankerous old man who was so negative his wrinkles had frozen into a frown?"

Jerry *knew* he had met several of these men. "Yes."

Larry continued, "The old man didn't become negative overnight. He *practiced* for many years. Similarly, the old woman didn't become pleasant overnight. She also practiced for many years. Does that make sense?"

Jerry nodded his head in agreement.

"Now, imagine these two from God's point of view. Can you imagine how pleasant a personality, and what a beautiful soul that old woman will have after she practices for ten thousand years? And can you imagine how *evil* the old man will be after he practices for ten thousand years?"

"It would be like living in the devil's land to be around him," Jerry shuddered.

"Exactly. Now you know why God insists that all those who will receive eternal life to be around Him must accept His Son as their Lord. Anyone who insists on his own way is trying to be an arrogant, selfish god, and the slightest character flaw will grow and grow, and that person will become unbearable to be around after they practice long enough. But those who accept Jesus as Lord are teachable. Given enough time and practice – which they will have – even the worst people can become pleasant companions *if* they will accept teaching. And the key to that is accepting that they owe everything to God, even life itself. Martha, I'd like a cup of ice water and two hot dogs with slaw." The pair had arrived at Martha's during Larry's talk.

"You know, when you put it that way, it begins to make sense why God wants us to worship Him. We have to accept our limits," Jerry mused.

"We have to accept that we were created by God for His purposes. And that means that we must think about the differences between Him and us. God isn't just a smarter, wiser version of us, you know. He's something completely 'Beyond.'"

Martha took Jerry's order. Jerry talked a bit with her about her business and family while the older man listened closely. As Martha went to fill the order, Larry spoke up. "Jerry, you did a fine job talking with her. She wants to tell you more, though. She has a big problem she needs to get off her chest."

"How do you know?" Jerry asked in shock.

"Everybody does. She doesn't attend a church because she thinks she's so busy. You'll need to stop by here someday between two and four when she's not so busy and she'll open up to you. And when she does, don't invite her to church. Yet. She needs to meet Jesus first, so instead of inviting her to church, tell her about Jesus and get her interested in what He offers first. Soon enough, she'll want to know more and start attending church."

"I will," Jerry promised.

Martha brought the two men their order. They paid and sat down at one of the picnic tables. After a couple of minutes, Jerry began to tell

Larry about the struggles he was having with the church. This time, though, Larry just listened.

After about thirty minutes, Larry stood to leave. "It has been a pleasure eating with you, Pastor. I hope we can do it again sometime."

Jerry stood and shook Larry's offered hand. "I'd like that. When can we get together again?"

"Oh, I figure I'll catch you after services in a couple of weeks."

"Great." Jerry turned back to pick up the trash on the table. When he turned around again, Larry was gone.

Discussion and Thought Questions

1) Is your church growing or shrinking?

2) What programs has your church tried recently?

3) If you asked people in your congregation, what would they say your church's mission was?

4) Why do you worship?

5) Name two points that Larry brought up that were new and different views for you. How do they differ from what you have believed in the past?

Chapter Three - Praising God

Jerry went home to his parsonage and collapsed on the couch. He was single – not by choice – but because he hadn't met the right girl. He started to turn on the television, but...something was bothering him. He couldn't get the things Larry had said out of his mind. He had always thought the purpose of the church was to fight for justice in the community and to be a safe place for people to come together in friendship to worship God. Nothing Larry said had contradicted any of that. But Larry talked about eternal life as though it were something naturally to be assumed. He talked about encounters with Jesus as though this was something that actually happened to people – not in a metaphorical sense. All of this was still churning in his mind as he fell asleep on the couch.

Jerry awoke with a start. He had had a fantastic dream. Jesus had been talking to him, showing him his little church packed full. And sitting in the front row were Larry and Martha. But Larry was dressed in a robe like those of Bible times. Martha had a kettle of hot dogs on her lap, telling him to "have another one. God has blessed them."

"That was odd," he thought.

Jerry sat down and looked up Matthew 28, the passage that Larry had quoted. It was the last chapter in Matthew's Gospel. He read it over and over, pulling out several commentaries and even looking up the passage on the Internet at biblegateway.com and checking several translations. Commentators called the passage "The Great Commission" and many large churches used it as their mission statement.

Jerry had, of course, heard the passage before, but he had forgotten about it. If what Larry was saying, it was the single most important command to the church. There was so much material about the passage that he decided that he would make it the focus of his sermons for the next month. He began to write in detail...

At the same time, across town, Shirley McDonald began to pray again. She prayed that the Holy Spirit would come upon her pastor this week as he wrote his sermon. She prayed that the sermon would express the will of God for her church. She prayed that her church would grow.

Three weeks later, Jerry was walking out of the church when Larry came up to him.

"How are things going?" Larry asked.

"I've been preaching on the Great Commission. I have another message planned for next week. People are starting to ask me how we can implement that mission in our little church. And some good news: two couples have come back. One man said I'd finally got on the right track." Jerry looked sheepish. "I guess I did get too involved in the mechanics of church and forgot the reason we do things."

"That's not a problem! Everybody gets off the rails from time to time." Larry was encouraging. "I figured it was about time for your second lesson."

"Great! Shall we walk over to Martha's for lunch?"

"Sure."

Larry walked for a minute in silence. Then he said, "You and your people now are beginning to understand what it is that church is about. Jerry, there are many, many people who have gone into the ministry these days who have lost sight of that, because many of the seminaries don't focus upon the Great Commission anymore. It used to be that the Great Commission was so widely known that almost everyone going to seminary was motivated by it, but over time the strategies that people used to get the attention of people in the world became the purpose of the church. For example, in the late 1800's and the early 1900's, people focused upon soup kitchens and urban mission homes so much that they became the purpose of the church – supporting the mission – rather than simply a strategy the church used to bring people to Jesus.

"Then later, especially during the civil rights movement of the sixties and later, justice causes took over many churches, as they used their moral strengths to fight against injustice in their communities. But as they spent time on those good social causes, they lost their focus on the need to bring people to the Lord first and foremost.

"And the same thing happened in the eighties and later as the church became associated with conservative political causes. In many ways, those were good causes, but many of those churches that went down that path lost their way and forgot how to bring people to Jesus, which is the only cause that makes a permanent, eternal impression in the Universe. You aren't the only pastor to make the mistake of assuming the cares of this world are more important than the eternal souls of the people of your community.

"By now, your congregation should know that the church has a God-given purpose which goes far beyond helping the poor, beyond social justice, beyond upholding standards of godly behavior, and beyond being a place to meet your friends on Sunday. The purpose of the church is to provide a place where Jesus Christ can change people's souls from their ugly selfish nature into souls that, given enough time, will be acceptable around our holy God. Jesus will accept them the way they are, but He has certain definite ideas about what the character of His followers should become. Hopefully, you and your people are beginning to realize this.

"The church is far more important than the Lion's Club or the Rotary or the Republican or Democratic Parties or the Sierra Club, for of all these, only the church concerns itself with things of eternal importance. Don't get me wrong – each of those clubs does important work. But they aren't in the same league because they are only concerned with the short term – the next ten or hundred years. In the church, we are concerned with eternity."

Jerry answered, "I never thought about it like that. I guess I've sold the church short, because we were trying to compete with some of those groups in the things we tried to do."

"That's right," said Larry. "You need to spend your time changing hearts eternally. If the hearts are changed, people will naturally form the groups to change the world. That's why you see such groups as The Salvation Army, Goodwill Industries, Catholic Charities, The Red Cross, and many, many hospitals. They were all formed by Christians who got the idea to change the world because they had listened to the Holy Spirit guiding them. That was what my friend Y'shua – excuse me, *Jesus* – was talking about when He called us salt and light for the world. You know, of course, that the name His friends and mother called Him was Y'shua, which is Aramaic for Joshua."

"Sure. Jesus was the Latin version of the name. Jesus was to be the new Joshua, leading the people into a new promised land."

"Good." Larry paused a moment. "The Spirit is telling me that the next thing you need to understand and teach your flock is how to evangelize."

"Oh, no. My people aren't evangelists." A vision of Billy Graham preaching in a stadium sprang into Jerry's head.

"Oh, yes, they are. They just don't know it. You and they probably think that evangelism is limited to Billy Graham-style 'crusades.' "

"Well, yes," admitted Jerry sheepishly.

"Most people think that or think about someone knocking on your door carrying a Bible. The word actually means to spread good news. But knocking on doors wasn't how the early church spread the word."

"How did they do it?"

"Let me see your Bible…. Acts chapter two, verses 42 through verse 47 says: *They devoted themselves to the apostles' teaching and to the fellowship, to the breaking of bread and to prayer. Everyone was filled with awe, and many wonders and miraculous signs were done by the apostles. All the believers were together and had everything in common. Selling their possessions and goods, they gave to anyone as he had need. Every day they continued to meet together in the temple courts. They broke bread in their homes and ate together with glad and sincere hearts, praising God and enjoying the favor of all the people. And the Lord added to their number daily those who were being saved.'*

"I always look to this section when I want to remember what a good healthy church looks like. Mind if I break it out for you?"

"Please do," replied Jerry.

Larry continued. "First, notice that the disciples were 'devoted' to the apostles teaching, to the fellowship, to the breaking of bread – that's communion and eating together – and to prayer. So they spent time together, ate together, studied the Bible and the commands of Jesus, prayed together and had communion regularly, perhaps every day.

"Next, they didn't care about who owned what. Even though there were over three thousand members of the Jesus Movement, they considered themselves to be a large family as far as possessions were concerned. Now, this wasn't a communistic society – the church didn't own everything, and nobody forced anyone to give up anything. People *voluntarily* gave to each other because they had learned that people were more important than possessions.

"Furthermore, they met together every day at the temple. They ate together in their homes. Now this next point is important. They *praised God.* Finally, everyone in town liked them and their numbers were growing daily. Are you with me?"

"Sure," Jerry replied. "They spent a lot of time together. But where's the evangelism program?"

"I'm getting to that. I think that where many of our churches have lost it is that they have become too focused on the big group program as the way to evangelize. The early church didn't have a program. What they did was very simple.

"They got together, studied Scripture, ate together, and praised God to their friends, neighbors, and family. The outreach and evangelism program was to simply *praise God!* How many times have you praised God to anyone outside your church walls this year? I know that I haven't heard you do it once."

Jerry was stunned. He hadn't praised God outside the church. In fact, he rarely praised God inside the church except in formal prayer. And his people didn't do it either. Of course, he didn't want to be seen as a religious nut!

"What about that old saying of showing Christ in our lives?" Jerry asked his older friend.

Larry smiled. "That is absolutely necessary. We must show Christ through our behavior and deeds. But it does little good if we never praise God. Let me give you an example.

"I go to the supermarket checkout line and let someone ahead of me. They thank me, saying something like, 'you're so nice'. What would you do with that compliment?"

"I'd say, 'thank you' and smile." Larry answered.

"I thought so. You've just taken glory from God. You *know* that you are naturally a mean, selfish person and you wouldn't be nice if it wasn't for the Holy Spirit in your heart. So instead of giving the credit to God – where it belongs – you've just taken credit for God's action."

"Ouch!" Larry understood. He enjoyed getting the praise of people – but he never pointed them back to God. "You're saying I should have said, 'thanks, but it is all because God changed me.'"

"That's right. Listen carefully." Larry ticked the numbers off on his fingers.

"One. If you praise God to your friends, neighbors, and family, they will begin to realize you know something about God."

"Two. When something happens in their life, they will think about you as a 'God-expert'. And you *are!*"

"Three. They'll ask you serious questions about God, which you can answer."

"Your people can do the very same thing. The typical person in our society knows very little about God and even less about Jesus Christ. Those people in your congregation have been listening to sermons for ten, twenty, fifty years. They truly are experts about God when compared to the ordinary public. And if someone asks them something too difficult for them, they can always come back to you for the answer, Pastor."

"So, they could all be praising God to their friends, neighbors, and family. That could really change things!" Jerry was getting excited.

"That's right."

One thing bothered Jerry. "Why don't we normally do this?"

Larry had anticipated the question. "Many pastors aren't secure in their position. They believe that everything must be done 'just right'. They don't truly believe that the Holy Spirit lives in all believers, and they are afraid to let their people run loose. Deep down, they are knowledge snobs and are afraid to share their knowledge and power. And so they don't teach their congregations to praise God outside the walls of the church.

"In addition, some churches have a tradition that only the ordained ministers or priests do the work of the church. But that is changing. Heck, even the Catholic Church made major changes encouraging more involvement by the laity in the 1960's, in the council known as Vatican II.

"The successful pastors are always teaching. They work to develop people step-by-step, giving them confidence that they were selected by God to spread the Gospel." Larry paused.

"There's another aspect of this you haven't asked me about."

"What's that?" Jerry asked.

"Nothing makes a person want to learn about the Bible more than someone asking him or her questions they can't answer. People who start praising God in public often get more involved in study.

"There is a long tradition of this. At one point, Jesus sent out seventy disciples in pairs to proclaim the Good News in a group of villages. Those disciples came back excited and asked questions of Jesus.

"If you can convince your people to regularly praise God to their friends, neighbors, and family, things will begin to happen in your church. You may need to start an apologetics study, a study about why we believe Christianity is true. And this "praising God" program is something that any church can do, small or large. Any individual can choose to do it even if the rest of the church doesn't get on board. It doesn't cost anything – except commitment to the church. And that's something your church has – otherwise those people would have also left."

"I'll try it." Jerry's eyes were wide open.

"Talk about it each week. It may take months before you see something, but something will eventually happen."

"All right." And with that, Larry took his leave.

Discussion and Thought Questions

1) When was the last time you praised God outside the church?

2) Why do you suppose more people don't praise God?

3) What are some simple ways you could praise God to others?

4) What scares you about praising God?

Chapter Four - Music Styles

Larry found his car. It was a small car, a Honda. He liked it because it operated cheaply. Not that he needed to save money on gas – his investments provided him much more than he needed to live on. But it was part of his personality now to be frugal. After so many years, living on little, fasting a lot, and always depending upon God for everything, Larry had learned how to live on very little and prided himself on being able to do so. It was his biggest vice and what he was working on. Pride.

He drove to the next town, where he planned to catch the gal that was the pastor at the Methodist church there. He had heard that she was having troubles similar to Jerry's troubles, but she was having the troubles for a different reason.

He saw Sarah going into the church as he drove past. He drove once around the block and parked. It began to rain as he walked quickly up the steps.

Once inside, the church was pleasant.

"Pastor Sarah!" he called.

The young woman in her late twenties came around the corner from an office. "Yes, how can I help you?" she asked.

"I've heard good things about you, and I wanted to meet you in person. I'm Larry." He held out his hand.

Sarah grabbed his hand and shook it solidly. She was friendly, but a bit suspicious. He decided to put her at ease.

"Jake Tomlinson was a good friend of mine, "Larry said. "He asked me to stop by after a year." Jake was the previous pastor at Sarah's church. He had died in office, two weeks after having a heart attack, and Sarah had taken his place, moving up from the associate pastor's position.

"Has it been a year already?" Sarah looked pensively. "I do miss the old fella."

"Jake knew that you'd do a good job, but that you might need someone to talk to after a year on the job. Jake and I went back many years together. So, when I saw him in the hospital, he asked me to stop in and see if you had any questions or issues going on that an old pastor could help with."

Sarah looked up at Larry. Her eyes briefly watered. "I guess he really knew what he was doing, for the last month I've needed someone to talk to. Things are beginning to fall apart here…"

Over the next hour the story came out. Sarah had been ready to modernize the church, ready to make changes now that Jake was gone. She had added a projector for computer slides and videos, started a new service at 9 AM with a praise band. She had reduced the number of scripture readings each Sunday from three to one and was using the newest book from the denomination for Bible Study, along with the newest hymnal from the denomination. But the changes she had put into place weren't working. In fact, people were starting to leave the church. She had just heard that three older women she loved and admired and had thought sick were actually attending the Baptist church down the street.

"Sarah, how do you feel about that?" Larry asked.

"Rejected, like my mom has thrown me out." She responded.

"Sarah, why did you change so many things?" Larry asked.

"I just wanted to make the worship more relevant for the younger generation. The older worship style is so dull and boring, and young people don't like it."

"But my dear, isn't this an older congregation?" Larry looked at her with compassion.

"Yes, but the church growth books all say to become relevant."

"Of course, they do. But isn't this also a town with few young people?"

"Well…yes."

"So, who is going to come into your new, relevant service? Who is this service relevant for?"

"Well…I guess there aren't many people. Just me, the praise band, and about ten people."

"You know, Sarah, I've found that praise bands and updated music often help churches. And I've also found that they often destroy churches. Do you want to know what makes the difference?"

"Yes, please." She looked like a little girl.

"Many pastors confuse the effect with the cause. People who already belong to a church don't come to a church because of the musical style. They come because they are part of a loving, trusting community with a purpose. Now, there are some churches that have as their purpose the perpetuation of their community. And others that have spreading the Gospel as their purpose. And still others believe that their purpose is to worship God or take care of each other or perform social services for the poor.

"Now, I happen to think that spreading the Gospel is the most important purpose. The Great Commission says that, and it sounds to me like you agree. But I'm not so sure that your people agree with that." Larry took a breath and continued.

"You see, when you implemented the new ideas, they remained *your* ideas. The people are still as cold toward outsiders as they ever were. They still don't believe that they are to spread the Gospel – and I'm not sure that you do either. I think that you believe that it is *your* purpose to spread the Gospel and *their* purpose to provide you with an audience." Larry looked hard at her.

Sarah blinked. A first a bit of anger showed in her face, and then a small wry smile appeared. "Larry – you're right. I have believed that. Thanks for pointing that out to me. I've been using them instead of training them."

"It takes a mature person to admit that, Sarah. I can see why Jake liked you so much."

Larry waved his hand around the sanctuary. "This place has a tendency to give people big egos. We have to be careful of that – all of us. But now, let me complete my thought.

"Sarah, the reason praise bands and new music work in some churches and destroy others is that the real issue is whether or not the congregation believes that the overall most important purpose of the church is to spread the Gospel. Those that believe that will do almost anything, gladly make almost any change, listen to any music, and generally crawl over broken glass on their naked bellies to get the Gospel to new people. If a praise band and new music will do it, they will support it fully.

"But those congregations that believe that the church is about taking care of *their* needs will never feel good about a change in worship style. They may 'allow' you to have a contemporary service or a seeker's service or a recovery service. But they will do so only if they can retain their comfortable church that continues to take care of them first and foremost. Congregations that are like this will complain about the 'balance' of resources between contemporary and traditional services, about each group getting their share of the pie. It makes board meetings sound more like Congress meeting to dole out money to each interest group than a group of people committed to spreading the Gospel."

"You're saying my congregation has different priorities."

"I'm saying your congregation hasn't committed to the Gospel Mission." Larry smiled back at her. "Yet."

"How do I get them to commit?" Sarah asked.

"Start with asking them to praise God to their friends and neighbors at least once a day."

Larry talked to her for about an hour about many of the same ideas from Acts 2 that he had talked to Pastor Jerry about. Then he said, "I've got to run, but I'll be back in a couple of weeks to help you with the next step."

And with that, Larry stood up and took his leave.

Discussion and Thought Questions

1. Does your congregation have a commitment to sharing the Gospel or are they focused upon taking care of themselves?

2. Give three examples that illustrate one view or the other.

3. To your congregation, is sharing the Gospel primarily the responsibility of the Pastor, the staff, an Outreach or Evangelism committee, the church as a whole or each individual person?

4. How would you schedule your pastor's week? How does his or her schedule actually work?

5. What is most comfortable about your church?

6. What is least comfortable about your church?

Chapter Five - Praises Galore!

Weeks had gone by. Jerry and Sarah were focusing their sermons on encouraging their congregations to praise God to their friends and neighbors. The message was in each sermon, the message was in each prayer, the message was even on the walls at Sarah's church – she had a banner made. Jerry's website and blog now asked people, "Have you praised God to a friend today?"

Donna Robinson attended Jerry's church. At first, she was confused and a bit frightened by the new message. But one day, while working at the checkout counter at Groceries-R-Us, she saw an opportunity. Jane Goodwin was looking glum when she came through Donna's line. Donna checked her out and said, "That'll be $9.01, please."

Jane looked through her wallet and handed Donna a ten-dollar bill. Rather than give her 99 cents in change, she took a penny from the cup and said, "Praise God that someone provided a penny for you."

Jane looked up. "Praise God? I guess we should praise Him for the little things. Thank you!" Jane had tears in her eyes.

What Donna didn't know was that about an hour before, Jane had found an old picture of her husband and her on their honeymoon that she hadn't seen in 20 years. Fred had died from lung cancer a year ago that morning.

Donna noticed the tears but decided not to say anything. The next customer was a young girl she didn't know. The girl had almost a dozen coupons. As she rang them up, she said, "Praise God someone decided to give us these coupons."

The girl responded. "Yes, indeed! It's the only way I could pay for them all." And she went on her way.

The rest of that day, she tried to find some way to praise God to each customer. Most responded in some way. A couple gave her an odd glance. But by the end of the day, she was feeling light and cheery – not tired and depressed like she normally did at the end of the day.

That evening, at Bible study, she told her story. Pastor Jerry cheered her on, and others complimented her.

The next day and every day for the rest of that month, she did the very same thing.

Jane came to her one day. "You know something about God, don't you?"

Donna was a bit surprised. But she answered, "I know He takes care of me."

Jane hesitated a minute. Donna continued, "Is there some way I can help you?"

Jane appeared to decide. "Donna, why do you think my husband was taken away at his age? He was only 56."

Donna stopped for a minute. "Mike! I need to take my break now!"

Donna walked Jane to a bench outside the store. As she walked, Donna said a quick prayer under her breath: "Lord, give me the words to say today." She motioned to Jane to have a seat.

"Jane, God is often hard to follow, but here's what I've learned about Him. First, He is good. He is so-o-o-o good. And that guides everything He does. Second, He always has a plan for us."

Jane looked down. "But Fred's plan ended last year. He had so much to do. He was my whole life. He was so good to me – he did everything for me, and I'm so lost without him."

Donna looked at Jane with compassion. "Did you ever think that God needed to remove Fred from you so you could grow?"

Jane began to sob. Her body shook. Donna pulled her close and held her...

They talked and cried for the next half hour. And then they met for dinner and talked and cried some more. And the next Sunday, Donna picked up Jane and they went to church together, for Donna had shown Jane Christ's wonderful Body in action and spoken the Word of God to Jane. And Jane believed.

Discussion and Thought Questions

1. Why do you think Jane talked with Donna?
2. What impact did praising God have on Donna?
3. Where and how can you praise God?
4. What did Donna do when Jane wanted to talk? How did she handle the conversation?

Chapter Six - A Listening Ear

Sarah was just beginning to give up hope of ever seeing Larry again when she found the dark, slim man standing on her church steps the Tuesday morning after Labor Day.

"Bet you thought I'd never be back," Larry said.

"Well – yes! I'm so glad to see you. Come in and let's talk," Sarah said.

She opened up the church and they went into the kitchen. Sarah made some coffee while they talked.

"Some people are beginning to praise God, but most are still the same as always. It's so discouraging." Sarah complained.

"Daughter, that's the way it always has been in the church. Even Peter had to deal with people who were more concerned with who got the handouts than with the Gospel mission. You remember the part in Acts where the Greek-speaking Christians complained about the distribution of bread to the widows, don't you?"

"Well, yes."

"How did Peter deal with it?"

"He appointed a group of trusted men that were Greek-speaking to handle the charity, while the Hebrew-speaking apostles continued to study the scriptures and teach people about Christ."

"That's right! He appointed people from the complaining group to handle the issue. And how did the Holy Spirit deal with it?"

"I'm not sure what you mean?"

"The Holy Spirit got involved, too. And the Spirit took those Greek-speaking men and used them in a mighty way. Stephen began preaching around Jerusalem and Philip later preached in Samaria and to the Ethiopian eunuch. Those men thought that they were signing up to distribute ordinary bread. But the Spirit led them to spread the knowledge of the Bread of Life!"

"So what are you saying?"

"I'm saying that you should get some of those grumblers involved in some sort of service project. If they will get their hands dirty taking food to some needy people in the community, they may get hit with the Spirit!"

"You see, Sarah, sometimes a person needs to *serve* before they will spread the Gospel. Many times, people are too focused upon themselves and need to get a taste of helping others before they can commit to anything further. So, we look for jobs for them to do. For example, you can start them out easy, letting them pass the plate during the offertory, or let them serve communion."

"Ok, I see." Sarah was warming to the matter. "But shouldn't the communion servers be qualified?"

"How much training does it take to teach a person to say, 'This is the Body of Christ, broken for you?', and to place a piece of bread in a person's hands? Really, some people have made that such an artificial position of honor. I like to use the position to get newer, more marginal people involved in the church. For example, if I need four people to serve – I always let others do most of the serving – I'll pick two men, two women, one who is older, one who is younger, one who is dressed nicely, and one who is dressed shabbily. That way, a message goes to the newer people that everyone gets involved in this church – it isn't a spectator sport!"

"But we've always had the same three people assisting me every month!" Sarah said.

"Yes, our problem is that people get stuck in specific jobs in the church. They become defined by them. So, we also need to move people around about once every few years to help them grow. Or, in the case of Communion server, change the people doing the job every time. To get someone involved, you might have someone simply put out the salt and pepper shakers at church dinners. Then, they begin to carry drinks to people. Later, they deliver food baskets to shut ins. Then, they do work for people who aren't in the church. Then, they begin more overt Gospel spreading. We have to encourage people to change jobs.

"But I have to warn you of something. People don't like being uncomfortable. And doing something new is always uncomfortable at first. People will complain, but they need to rotate jobs. Sometimes, we just have to let someone fail at a position before they will let someone else work that job without criticism.

"I once had a scripture reader who went through some hard times. So, I asked her to step aside for a few months to work through her issues. During that time, I let 20 different people read scripture, including those who were most critical of her. After people read scripture, they appreciated the work of the people who did it regularly. But you do have to give people the chance to say 'no.'

"Now, I have one other thing I need to teach you. Can you meet me tomorrow afternoon out at Eve's Apple Farm around 2 pm?"

"Well, yes, "Sarah replied. "Why?"

"I have a special thing I need to show you."

"I'll be there, "Sarah answered.

She sat and thought for a moment. Then she asked, "Larry, where are you from? How do I get in touch with you?"

Larry smiled back at her. "Daughter, I am originally from the Holy Land, but now I just travel. My wife and I have our own ministries – we travel all over the place. You can send me an email when you need me."

Larry wrote down his email address, thanked her, and left.

It was much later that evening when she looked at the email address as she was typing it into her computer. L@bethanystinker.org.

"Bethany's tinker? I wonder what that means." She copied it into her phone's email program and went home to bed.

Discussion and Thought Questions

1. Does your church rotate jobs or do people stagnate in a single position for years?

2. Is there any clear progression of ministry training jobs for new people in your congregation?

3. How could your congregation better deal with complainers?

Chapter Seven - The Apple Farm

Sarah arrived at the apple farm to find Larry waiting for her. After greetings, he led her up into the orchard.

It was a warm, early September day with a gentle breeze. Birds were chirping in the distance. A turkey buzzard circled high overhead. Every couple of minutes, a loudspeaker on Eve's barn let off the sound of a red-tailed hawk. Red and yellow apples were glowing through the deep green foliage on either side of them as they went deeper into the orchard.

Larry led Sarah to the Golden Delicious trees. He carefully found two plump apples. "Here, take this one, it's delicious."

Sarah looked at the apple. Then she looked closer at the apple. "I'll need to wash this first before I can eat it."

Larry looked back at her with a grin and a gleam in his eye. "I knew you'd say that."

Sarah looked puzzled. "But there's dirt on this apple."

Larry smiled. "Those black specks are what farmers call flyspeck or sooty blotch. It is a harmless fungus that grows on Eastern apples. Farmers have a simple way of dealing with it. Rub it on the leg of your jeans." And Larry did just that with his apple. "Then eat."

Sarah hesitated but slowly and carefully did the same. She took a bite.

Warm honey flavored with citrus flowed into her mouth. It was the most delicious apple she'd ever eaten!

Larry smiled at her. "Western apples are what you find in supermarkets. They're bred to withstand the long railcar journey and to succeed in supermarkets. They have much better color – and tougher skins – but they don't have the *taste* of these apples. Western apples are also coated with a thin layer of harmless wax to keep them from drying out and to make them shine under bright supermarket lights. They have to be picked before they're fully ripe or they'll go bad on the trip, so they aren't as sweet as apples that are left on the tree until fully ripe. Plus, as soon as the apple is picked, the juice begins to dry out. And so Western apples often have thick skins and taste dry and starchy by the time we get them.

"On the other hand, these apples are perfectly ripe. They taste the way that God intended, and we're eating them the way God intended – as a son and a daughter of Adam picking them off the tree.

"Yet, you were concerned with dirt."

Sarah looked at him. "What about bacteria and dirt and pesticides?"

Larry continued. "Eve sprays pesticides on these apples to reduce the fungus and the worms. If she didn't spray, there'd be no way to get you apples. Here in Ohio, we live in a warm, moist climate – unlike the apple-growing region of eastern Washington State. There, they don't get much rain in the summer – they irrigate from mountain snows that melt into the rivers. You see, every drop of water on the skin of an apple gives fungus a chance to get started. That's where those little black specks come from. It can't be avoided in the East – but that fungus is completely harmless – it just means the apple isn't as pretty as one that was grown in the West.

"Eve sprays in the spring but stops spraying in June. She only uses the gentlest pesticides because she wants to eat these apples too. After three months of rain drenching the apples, the pesticides are long gone. And after the hot sun of August, any bad bacteria have been scorched and sunburned to death. If an hour or two in August sun will give you a sunburn, what do you think days of sun will do to little bacteria?

"But there's a lesson to be learned here."

"What's that? "Sarah continued to eat her apple.

"Too many people today are concerned about dirt. People who ate mud pies when they were four-years old, people whose grandparents washed the udder of their own cow and drank the warm milk unpasteurized, people whose great-grandparents slaughtered pigs outside and hung them up in a tree to drain, people whose ancestors bent over inside a chicken coop to gather eggs are concerned about the least little dirt in their food. Even the allergists tell us that one cause of allergies is too little exposure to dirt as a child."

"But what does this have to do with my congregation?" Sarah was beginning to wonder if the older man had spent too much time in the sun.

"We like our visitors washed before they come into the congregation, just like you wanted that apple washed before you ate it. "

"Oh!" Sarah saw the connection.

"'Oh' is right, young lady." Larry looked at her. "We want our visitors to be clean, to not cuss, to not have tattoos, to be polite, to not be angry, to not use drugs, alcohol, or tobacco, to not have any messy mental problems, to be pleasant people – before we let them into the church. We want them to look good, to have thick skins, to be predictable in their flavor. People from outside the church are full of juice, they have strong flavors, and they have fungus on them that keeps us from getting to know them, from *tasting* them. And they have thin skins. Always remember that unchurched people have thin skins and they are easily bruised and damaged, like Eastern apples. Yet, how will they ever improve if they aren't in the church?

"Sarah, we are to wash people *after* they come to church. We wash people after Jesus has connected with them and they've accepted that first washing by His blood. We wash people by baptism only after they've had a chance to desire their hearts to change. Yet, your people, deep down, only want nice clean Christians to come to the church. They want to keep a closed, clean, anti-septic environment, the same way they want perfectly clean food."

"You're so right! My congregation really doesn't want messy people. They only really want other Christians to join them." Sarah agreed quickly.

"But don't be too hard on them, Sarah. That's the way people normally are. It is very, very difficult to accept people who are very mixed up. Jesus was the only person that I know that could accept everyone. For example, I have a real problem with people who like the band *Queen*, which I think wrote some of the worst music ever. They were nowhere as good as *Aerosmith*," Larry joked.

"I have my own issues," Sarah said. "Yet, I try to put them aside so that people will come to the church…How can we overcome this problem?"

"It is very difficult. You will need to preach a bit about the issues we've talked about, but it won't be enough. This is where your second service is really a life saver. Go back and focus upon your traditional service for your regular people but begin to develop a really different service for the people in town who need help. You might want to encourage AA or similar groups to meet at the church midweek, and then begin to hold a recovery service for the people of those groups on Friday nights. You can bring people with you to minister in the rough parts of town.

"Or, "Larry continued, "You might want to start a completely different service, even with a different language for the immigrants in the community. Although you might seed these different services with key people from your main service, don't expect everyone to adopt the idea. Instead, spend your persuasion time convincing people that everyone should be welcome at your church. Bring in some visiting speakers that are deep spiritually but look very different. Get your people used to others gradually."

"Thanks!" Sarah was smiling. "Can I have another apple?"

Discussion and Thought Questions

1. How representative of your community is your church? Think about ethnic groups, economic groups, and age groups.

2. What groups of people do you wish were better represented?

3. What groups of people do you have a problem relating to?

4. How could you get to know some of the people you don't like or know very well?

Chapter Eight - Four Fences

Donna still attended Jerry's church. Over the last few months she had praised God to many people and had begun helping all sorts of people.

One day, she was leaving the grocery store when Jerry and Larry walked up. "This is the woman I've been telling you about, Larry. Donna has quite a ministry going. Donna, this is Larry – he gives me advice about the ministry and wanted to meet you."

"Nice to meet you, Larry." Donna wondered who this Larry guy could be.

"Donna, could we have a cup of coffee together? Larry has a couple ideas and a story he wants to tell you."

"I...I suppose so. Let's go to Café Brown."

They made small talk while they walked a minute or two, ordered their coffees and sat down.

Larry began, "I hear you've been talking to people about God."

"Well, I guess I have been," Donna responded nervously.

"That's fantastic!" Larry said. "I wish more people would talk about Jesus and God. Too many people are keeping their mouths shut."

Donna relaxed. "I just try to listen to them and tell them how God can help them."

"That's the way to do it. Are you making a difference?"

"Yes, I think I am. Several people come back to me each week and tell me what's happening in their lives."

"You know, you might want to consider inviting several of your regulars over to your home for a party. And be sure to invite Pastor Jerry to come over, too. You might just get a regular Bible study out of that party, and it might be all that a couple of people need to finally come to the Lord," Larry looked at her.

"Oh, I don't know that I have the training or anything to lead a Bible study. "Donna actually began to blush! She hesitated for a minute, then began again.

"There are some of the people that I would like to lead to the Lord, but I can't seem to get anywhere with them. It's like they just dismiss me out of hand."

Larry smiled knowingly. "There are several fences that people have to cross before they can come to the Lord. Let's look at them:

"The first fence is trust. Before anyone will listen to what you have to say, they have to trust you. And many people in our society have been hurt by church people, or they have absorbed what Hollywood says about Christians, that we are mean, hate-filled people."

Donna jumped in: "I know what you mean. I know a few people who almost run when I mention God."

"That's right. In most cases, those folks have never met a genuine committed Christian who has worked on becoming personally holy. And so, you simply need to do Christian acts of kindness for them. In short, to be trusted, you need to show that you are trustworthy. What makes people trustworthy?"

Donna thought a moment. "Well, they're honest, they're reliable. They don't tell secrets. They listen before answering and when they answer, their advice is sound. And they don't talk about other people."

"You're right! Those are some traits of trustworthy people. I'm sure that you can think of more if you think about it."

Jerry spoke. "I'm sorry to say, but I often judge people's trustworthiness by their clothing, their personal appearance, and their demeanor. I trust people who project stability and seriousness more."

Donna responded. "I don't know – I'm more likely to trust someone who is open and jokes with me. I don't trust people who wear suits – they're too full of themselves."

Larry stepped back in. "You notice that trustworthy means different things to different people. In general, there are certain common aspects, though. Trustworthy means that you are a friend who is similar in important ways to you, and most importantly, you are predictable and act in my best interests – and you won't sell me out for a cheap thrill of gossip or any other reason."

Donna listened. "I see what you mean. Jerry dresses conservatively, so he prefers people who dress conservatively. I'm pretty open and talkative, so I prefer people who are open and talkative."

Larry came back. "That's right. And the first fence that everyone has to cross is the fence of trust. Until they make it over that fence and join you on this side, they will not listen to anything you have to say about Christ."

Jerry put in. "Is that why so many of the books talk about building relationships first?"

"Exactly. A good relationship is a trusting relationship." Larry was ready to move on. "Now let's look at the second fence.

"Our second fence that people have to cross to come to Christ is the fence of need. In their journey to Christ, everyone has to see a real problem in their life. People who don't have a problem don't see a need for Christ. And people who believe they can solve all of their problems won't see a need for Christ.

"There are some people who don't believe they have any problems. Usually, these are the more worldly successful people...Men and women who are experiencing failure are much quicker to turn to Christ for help than those who win at everything. So it is our task to help people see and face the problems they cannot solve alone head-on."

Jerry asked, "So, what are you saying?"

Larry continued. "Many people can point directly at their problem, but they often point to the symptoms of the real problem. Let me give you an example...

Donna and Jerry looked at each other as Larry took a drink from his coffee mug.

"Let's say you are upset because you have lost your job. Why are you upset?"

Donna answered. "That's easy. You're afraid you can't pay your bills."

Larry continued. "But why are you upset because you can't pay your bills?"

Jerry took a turn. "Because you will get tossed out of your house and you won't be able to buy food."

Larry led them. "And what's wrong with losing your house or not being able to buy food?"

Donna jumped at it. "You'll be homeless, freeze to death and starve." She looked up. "You'll die!"

Larry smiled a broad grin. "You've got it. Fear of death is behind almost all fears. And if you ask your friend 'why' about five times in a row, you will almost always find out from them that their real fear, their real problem is a fear of death. And you know what? No one has a good answer for death – except Jesus Christ."

Jerry was excited. "You're saying that the fear of death underlies all of our other fears and if we help people see that they have no answer for the problem of dying, they must begin to look for Christ?"

"Exactly. No matter what a person's problem is – as long as they are sane – the root fear that makes that problem become an important problem to them is the fear of death – because that is a problem no one can solve. Except Jesus."

Donna asked, "What if they are afraid of their mother dying...Oh! That fear makes them realize they can't solve death for themselves. "

"That's right. So, if we ask the 'why's' and help the person come to face his or her fear of death, we can begin to talk intimately and deeply about Christ and what Christ did for us." Larry looked up, flagged down the waiter, and ordered a refill of his coffee.

Jerry looked at Larry. "You mentioned four fences. What are the other two fences that keep us from Christ?"

Larry began again. "The third fence everyone must cross is the fence of help. Everyone must see why Christ helps them with their need. And this is the fence that we so often try to get people to immediately, but that never works. You see, if a person doesn't trust us, and they don't see a need for Christ, then telling them what Christ will do for them is useless."

Donna waved her hand. "Oh, Oh. It's like they've still got their britches caught on the barbed wire of the trust fence or the need fence and we're trying to help them over the help fence."

"Ha-ha! That's a colorful way of putting, and very true. You can't help people over the fence of help until they have decided they trust you and have a problem they can't solve without Christ." Larry's eyes were sparkling with joy.

"When you get to the fence of help, it is easy if you've prepared the way earlier, helping your friend cross the first two fences in order. But sometimes, they need to go back to the trust fence for a while, because the idea that Christ can help is sometimes difficult for someone to swallow, especially if they've been committed to a godless Universe."

"So how do you build that trust with them?" Jerry wanted to know.

"You'll need to be ready with sober, personal stories of when Jesus helped you in your life. You need to tell those God-stories of yours without exaggeration, without embellishment. You need to be an exact witness, telling them what you saw, what you prayed for, what happened, what you saw, heard, felt, and even smelled or tasted if it is relevant. In short, you need to tell them a story about how God helped you. Or several stories. God has helped you in your life, right?" Larry asked them mischievously.

"What if they still don't believe?" Jerry pushed.

"They probably *won't* believe right then and there. But that's ok. This is not a fifteen-minute process. We're playing for the long term.

"Some people, you see, are very committed to a worldview which tells them that God cannot exist. And these people may have some serious questions that need to be answered... questions about Genesis, questions about miracles, questions about the validity of the Bible.

"For these people, there are several answers you can provide.

"First, I generally explain to the people hung up fighting a seven-day creation or other aspects of early Genesis that many Christians debate these issues, also. Honestly, if someone is hung up on Genesis, you cannot win them for the Lord, no matter how many facts of creation science you debate with them, for they have many facts also and the support of the scientific establishment. Instead, we need to bring them back to Christ. Believing in Christ being divine is the key – Genesis is something to work out later after a person accepts Christ and has the benefit of the Holy Spirit in his or her life.

"Now I'm not saying that God didn't create the world in seven days – and I'm not saying God did create the world in seven days or seven billion years. What I am saying is that the answer to that question is ultimately irrelevant to whether Jesus Christ was and is the Son of God – with all that implies – because many wise, solid, Bible-believing Christians have chosen both sides of the issue. I wasn't there – I'm not 100% sure what the answer is. But I am certain that you cannot bring a soul to Christ by arguing the point with a committed evolutionist. All we do by arguing this point directly is make the person we are trying to bring to Christ into our debating opponent, which keeps them away from Christ. And so we need to move the argument away from Genesis and into John."

"And what about the miracles?" Jerry asked.

"There are only three approaches to miracles. Either they happen, they might happen, or they can't happen by definition. If your friend is taking the last position, then he is very closed-minded and is arguing from a dogmatic philosophy rather than using the scientific method. You see, a real scientist would keep an open mind and allow that miracles might exist – or not. Their presence would be evidence that the supernatural exists. Encourage him to consider this."

"And the validity of the Bible?" Donna asked.

"That is a subject which is too long for this talk and there are at least two excellent books on the subject. *The Case for Christ* by Leo Strobl and *Know Why You Believe* by Paul D. Little. Get a copy of one or the other or both and read it.

"In short, there is evidence from historical records, archeology, psychology, literary analysis, individual testimony, and the internal evidence of the Bible which indicates that the Gospel stories are true. Jesus taught that His followers will receive eternal life, He was executed for claiming to be God, and He rose from the dead, proving He was divine, and proving God's love for us."

Donna thought for moment. "I'll get one of the books. But what is the last fence?"

"The last fence is the fence of hurry. People may trust you, they may understand they can't beat death, they may know that Christ holds the key to eternal life. But for some reason, they believe they have all the time in the Universe before they commit.

"The core reason is they are intelligent people. Intelligent people recognize that admitting that Christ is divine means that they must admit they are not divine, that they are not in control, and that they must bow the knee to another. And that is not a decision that pure reason can make. They must want to bow down, to face the embarrassment of telling their friends and family that they are now Christian, to admit that they aren't as all together as they have been claiming. And so they take time.

"Our job is to remind them that they might die at any time and then it will be too late. People really do get hit by buses." They all looked toward the street, where a large bus had stopped and was idling in front of the coffee shop. Silence filled the booth as they contemplated the invisible figure of Death.

Discussion and Thought Questions

1) Describe a conversation you had recently with an unbeliever.

2) Which fence are your friends, neighbors, and family stuck behind?

3) What fence was most important for you when you came to Christ?

4) How much do you think about death?

Chapter Nine - The Pastor of Taco Bell

Donna was quiet for a minute. "That helps. That helps a lot. But I'm still not sure that I've got what it takes to lead a Bible study."

Larry looked at her with a smile for a long minute. Then he said to her:

"Donna, I want to tell you a story about a friend of mine in another state who had something similar happen to her. It might give you some ideas for your ministry."

"OK. I'll listen."

Larry began to tell the story. "I call the story, *The Pastor of Taco Bell*. Let me get into it."

He paused and his eyes went far away. He began to speak…

…She walked into the Taco Bell one afternoon. Her silver-gray hair was cut short in a "cute" manner. She was about five-foot-five and weighed… well, it was a bit above optimum. Her doctor kept asking her to lose weight. She nervously went to the counter and asked, "Excuse me, could I have an application?" The girl behind the counter handed her the application, almost without looking up.

The woman, who carried a large purse in which there was a recent AARP card, took the application with a gentle smile and went to the corner table to fill in the blanks. For the last fifteen years she had worked in her and her husband's business, but the business had declined recently, and she needed money to pay off some business debts. He was already working three other jobs – teaching at both a private Catholic high school and at a Church of Christ college in the evenings, and pastoring not one, but two Methodist churches, while also attending seminary full-time online. Money was short, but God was good. God always provided if you sought His kingdom first.

She filled in the application and took it to the counter. The boy, wearing a tag that read "Assistant Manager", was in his early twenties. He took the application and said, "Just a minute." She waited in her J.C. Penney-bought outfit. Her face was just a little pink – she sometimes had rosacea attacks – and there were smile wrinkles just beginning to form around her eyes, which were small but laughing behind her glasses. A touch of black ink was on her fingers from filling a bottle with ink – the business her husband had started and that she ran. She hadn't noticed, but there was a slight trace of flour on her elbow where she had made biscuits that morning for her husband and the two children that were still at home. She had homeschooled them and an older son who towered above her. He was away at a private college on a good scholarship. The two older girls had families of their own. A tiny piece of curled white hair was on her skirt, courtesy of her little Shih Tzu puppy that guarded the house from the mailwoman.

"Are you Josie?" the woman walked up to her and asked. Her nametag read "Barbara".

"Jessie", she replied.

"I'm Barbara, the manager. Do you have time for an interview now?"

"Of course," Jessie responded.

"Let's go over to the corner table." The thirty-something woman led the way confidently to the corner.

They sat down. "Tell me about your work experience," Barbara began.

Jessie began, "I've mostly been in sales and I know how to work." She continued to tell her the details of the jobs she had worked at. The glove factory where she always sewed at bonus levels, the IV drug factory where she was asked to supervise, but her first husband wouldn't let her. The newspaper ad sales job that let her get free from his terrorism and control. The insurance job where she had been the top rookie. The Radio Shack job and the second newspaper ad job and the second insurance job and the glorious two years when she had run her family daycare business in New Jersey and made top dollar because she knew children and the daycare business allowed her to stay home with the son she thought she'd never have. She didn't mention that it allowed her time to study her cooking and fix gourmet-quality dinners for her second husband.

She told her about the move to Atlanta and joining her husband in his first business, which failed, but the growth of the second business which had paid the bills for over a decade. She told her about answering the phone and taking customer orders at all hours, that the most important part of any business was the customer. But she skipped the parts where they prayed and prayed and prayed to God for funds to stay in business and how He always granted those prayers, but eventually moved her husband out of the business to teach and then to preach.

"I will need Sundays off because I'm a pastor's wife and the congregations expect me to be there. And there's one more thing you need to know. I won't be working for Taco Bell. I'll be working for God. He demands that I do my best at all times, so I will always be working to please Him." She concluded.

"You seem to know customer service. You know, we have a lot of younger kids that need an example. Please join us. I think we need you here," Barbara responded. "When can you start?"

"I've got another interview at the Mall this afternoon. I'll let you know this evening." They talked for a few more minutes about salaries and uniforms, and about their children. And then she left.

The other interview also went well. It was 30 minutes farther travel but paid an extra fifty cents per hour. That evening, she talked it over with her husband.

"I think you'll use up the extra money in gas and food," he said. "But more importantly, I think you'll have a ministry at the taco place." And with that advice, she called Barbara back and said she'd take the job.

She started on Tuesday afternoon and it was difficult. Barbara put her on the money collection drive-through window. The hardest part was reading back the orders from the little short codes that were printed on the screen. In a world with icons and iPads, with voice-recognition software and smart phone apps, Taco Bell chose to make their employees memorize arcane codes such as "TS-L" for "Soft Taco, hold the lettuce." There were over 60 product codes. When she, who had set up her invoicing system and prepared her web pages, asked for a product listing, she was told that none existed. So she began developing her own listing to study.

Even more troubling was the front register. Instead of icons or even full English words, the system used those little codes. To place an order required her to go two and sometimes three levels down in the order entry system. And there didn't seem to be any rhyme or reasons to the structure of the menus. She came home and cried to her husband.

But good things began to happen almost immediately. Her first night, three kids came back from the grill line and began loudly talking: "f--- this! f--- her!" back and forth. She said to the older man in the car at the window: "One moment, please!", closed the window, turned her back to the window and yelled, as only a mother of five can yell: "KNOCK IT OFF! The customers can hear you!"

Silence…

She turned back to the window, opened it and said, "Now, sir. Was your order a soft taco plain, two chicken quesadillas, and a medium Pepsi?" He grinned and nodded.

It took a couple of weeks, but the harsh language disappeared, first around her window, and then throughout the store.

Meanwhile, she made friends. She decided that the Taco Bell would be her congregation and she would be the pastor. So she hugged the girls and complemented the boys. She cheered up the grouchy guy her age and gave the young managers advice on raising their kids. She showed one girl how to clean trays in a flash and showed a boy why the sanitizing solution had to be hot. Her window area began to gleam as she put vinegar on the lime buildup at the sink, and she learned the codes. She mentioned God a couple of times a day.

The employees were mean with each other. They gossiped continually and made terrible, off-color jokes about each other. They called each other names that would get any politician's resignation in five minutes flat. And they didn't have any concept of how to be nice to each other. Jessie showed them and gradually talked to each of them about the name-calling and the jokes and the damage they were doing with it. And she showed them another way by her kindly, gentle example. Over the course of a month, "niceness" grew at the Taco Bell.

As customers came to the window in the evenings, she used her charm on them. "That's a beautiful car," she told the owner of the shiny red Firebird. He beamed back. "I love your puppy," she said to the owner of the Rottweiler that was barking at her. "Your baby is so cute" she said to the young mother struggling with the infant in the car seat.

Barbara came to her. "You are leading the store in call-backs," she said.

"What are those?" Jessie asked.

"That's when people call the number on the receipt to tell us who is doing a good job. Keep it up!"

Meanwhile, she continued to train the youngsters she worked with in how to be nice to each other. She gave hugs and loaned her counterfeit-marking pen to them "Remember to bring it back!" And they did, because they loved her and respected her.

They tried to shock her by telling her about their pot-smoking and she told them about her friends that smoked pot when she was young. She often put in a gentle, very gentle comment about how her friends had either stopped and turned out well, or not stopped and not turned out well. The comments were never preachy, just "lessons an old woman has learned". And she hugged them.

One evening, a seventeen-year old girl was in a huddle with tears with two of her friends. Jessie could just hear snatches. "They'll give you the abortion and your parents will never know." … "It won't cost you anything!"

Jessie caught the girl's eye. She motioned with her index finger to "come here!"

The girl came over. Her eyes were red. Jessie gave her a hug. "Let me tell you about a place run by some friends of mine. They'll give you a free ultrasound, they'll help you with diapers and formula, and they'll even help you with a crib and other equipment. They have contacts with people that want to adopt – or they'll help you raise your baby if you want. You DO have options." And the whole story came out. Jessie listened – she had heard it before. A great hot guy, she gave in, he got what he wanted, and then he left as soon as he heard the news. Jessie hugged her again. She told her that in the Bible, when God wants to bless a woman, He gives her a child. It was a regular sermon. A couple days later the girl told her she had decided to keep the baby. Jessie sent up prayers of thanksgiving that evening.

The young boy that had taken her application found out his girlfriend was pregnant. Jessie prayed and talked with him. Two weeks later, he announced that he was getting married to the girl in a month or so.

The grouchy guy smiled when she talked to him. She actually caught him singing while he was working once. "Don't tell anyone," he said. "I've got a reputation to think about."

One of the girls called her one day at home. She was terribly sick and needed to go to the hospital, but her boyfriend, a trucker, was in Florida. Jessie went and took her to the hospital and stayed with her until midnight and then visited her the next day. She prayed with her and helped her until her boyfriend was able to help her. They started to attend one of her husband's churches.

Her ministry grew. Everyone at the Taco Bell knew she was a pastor's wife. Everyone knew she was a Christian – such as the bi-sexual boy she was fast becoming friends with until he was fired. She wept that night.

Workers came and went – there's a lot of turnover in fast food. But each of them got Jessie's smile and hugs, her gentle advice and prayers – even the prisoner on work-release. Customers came into the drive-through tired and went away smiling from her jokes. The drive-through line seemed to get a little longer each Friday evening. People came by just to see her at the window. She began to get tips.

But one day, she had a doctor's appointment. The verdict was surgery and no work for six weeks. So she had to leave.

She told the older grouchy guy who wasn't so grouchy anymore. She said, "But I'll be back to visit."

"Lord, I hope so." he said and looked pained.

The girls hugged her and the young male manager that was getting married had tears in his eyes. And she left.

But a couple of weeks before that, after talking to her husband, Jessie called up the Methodist District Superintendent. "Bill," she said, "I want to be a pastor." She told him of her experiences.

"We'll start the process right away," he said.

And while she recovered from her surgery, she began reading about the job she already knew how to do.

{Based upon a true story}

"Well, what do you think?" Larry asked.

Donna *and* Pastor Jerry were both in tears.

Donna spoke first. "I guess you're telling me that I need to completely consider myself a pastor for the people at the store."

"I'm not saying anything. That's for you and the Lord to work out together. And from everything Jerry's been telling me, you and He are not strangers." Larry grinned at her.

"Donna, if you want to get more training, I can arrange it," Jerry offered. "Although I'm not really sure what you need."

"I don't know. Sometimes I really wish I knew more church history and sometimes I need an answer why we believe in some things."

"Such as...?" Jerry prodded.

"Such as why we take communion and what the difference is between Hinduism and Buddhism, why our God is different from Allah, and any reasons not in the Bible for the existence of God."

"WHOA! That's quite a list, lady." Larry stopped her.

"I know, but sometimes I feel like I just need more answers."

"Have you ever *not* been able to help someone?" Larry asked.

"No. I've always been able to help people understand God better, and the Holy Spirit has always given me the words to say. But I just feel unprepared." She smiled at the men.

Larry smiled back. "That, my dear, is the way we all are. Oh, yes. We need to read books and books and more books. It sounds like you want books on apologetics like Paul D. Little's *Know Why You Believe*, or Lee Strobel's *The Case for Christ*. But you'll find that the important answers are given to you by the Spirit if you are in constant quiet prayer when talking to someone. That how "Jessie" did it at Taco Bell. She always prayed for help."

"Was she real?"

"Yes. And she's directly responsible for about a dozen people coming to the Lord and indirectly responsible for hundreds more. And she hasn't even completed seminary yet."

"I hope I can be like that."

"You can. I've seen your type before. Keep following the Lord and you will harvest many souls, sister. "Larry gave her a confident look. Softly, "I'm not saying your life will be easy, but it will be fulfilling. You will always have friends, too."

At that, the coffee ran out and the three dispersed. Larry looked after Donna and said a quiet prayer. "Lord, protect her in this time of testing. Bless her beyond measure – as you have blessed me. But do not put her through the testing that I underwent. In the name of Jesus, I pray. Amen."

Discussion and Thought Questions

1. What struck you most about Jessie's story?

2. What was her approach to life?

3. How did she treat the people at the Taco Bell?

4. What could you do to imitate her?

Chapter Ten - The Council

Jerry was feeling good. Things were beginning to change subtly at the church. Donna and a few other people were getting the idea that praising God was their personal mission. And it was beginning to tug at the church.

However, there was one problem. The problem was that several members of the church council weren't getting the message. At the last meeting, things just didn't seem right, and he couldn't put his finger on it. And that's why he was so glad when Larry had called him up and asked to meet him at the coffee shop the day before the next meeting.

Larry was waiting for him when he arrived. After the usual pleasantries, Jerry got down to business and explained the problem he was having with the church council.

"They seem to treat the council like they're running the school board or like it is a city council meeting. They're always jockeying for political power and working to get things their way."

"Are they committed to the Mission?" Larry asked.

"That's the problem. I don't think that they really care about the mission. I think that they're just focused upon managing me."

"Have you led them into that position?"

"What do you mean? I don't even have a vote on the council. I don't lead them anywhere. It's their church and they know it. They know I'll be gone in a couple of years, so they run the show." Jerry was puzzled.

"Pastor, because of your position, God has appointed you to lead this church. It doesn't matter what the church constitution says. People will look for you for leadership. Can you imagine any governor or any President that wouldn't give his eyeteeth to have the opportunity to talk to everyone for twenty to thirty minutes once a week?"

Jerry thought a minute. "I guess I kind of control the agenda, don't I? What I say from the pulpit will guide the people more than what the council does, won't it?"

"Exactly! They can adjust budgets around all that they want, put money in one bucket and take it out of another, give money for dinners and take it away from advertising, but ultimately, what you tell the people from the pulpit will change the church. The council has little direct power if the individual people run with the ball."

"But I'd like them to get on board so we can use their influence..."

"Use your own. They'll come on board when they listen to the Holy Spirit, same as everyone else. The only thing you can do is to insist upon a prayer and devotional time at council meetings and use that time to reinforce the message. Praise God! Teach the Mission!"

"But I was sort of hoping to get a computer projector this month."

"You don't need it. Just tell them that one day the church might want to consider such a purchase, but don't worry yourself and them over it. You still don't get it, do you?"

"I have a feeling you're going to tell me what I don't get, aren't you?" Jerry smiled at Larry.

"Yes. You still think that the keys to church growth are programs and technology and music and stuff. They aren't. It's people who are committed to spreading the Gospel! And that's *not* the same as inviting people to church." Larry was on a roll. "You're like Martin Luther – you have a hard time making a break with the past. If it was up to him, the Reformation would have never happened. He was forced into his stand. But the real energy for the Reformation came from Switzerland, where Calvin and Zwingli were ready to make a complete break with the old ways of doing things. Mind you, they weren't always right in their ideas, but they had the energy. If Luther's hand hadn't been forced, little would have changed.

"In the Book of Acts, there were many people who heard and gave lip service to the new ideas of Christ but were not ready to listen to the Holy Spirit. John wrote about those who were still fighting a rearguard action decades later when the seven letters to the churches in Revelation were written. Many people held to Jewish customs and insisted that you must become Jewish first before you can become Christian. But others didn't believe so. Peter and Paul led that change. And so gradually, the gentile churches began to outstrip the conservative churches in membership and vitality. By 150, most of the "Jewish-first" churches were dying out. But the gentile church was growing rapidly. I remember on Cyprus when..." Larry stopped abruptly and then continued.

"Don't worry about your projector or your music, son. It'll come. But first, help the Holy Spirit change the hearts of your council." Larry concluded.

Jerry thought for a moment. Deep down, which did he think would work, the technology or praising God? He relaxed.

"I guess churches grew before there were projectors," he told Larry. "I won't even bring it up unless someone else does. I'll just teach a bit more on the Great Commission.

"That's the way! I have confidence in you, son." Larry was grinning. "Don't worry – there'll come a time when they will ask for a projector. And a praise band. But until then, focus upon getting them to praise God.

"Jerry, leading a church to grow isn't a quick thing. It took Jesus three years to prepare His disciples to be apostles – and He was with them twenty-four-seven in the flesh! Here's a rough timeframe that I've found works.

"Your first year, a new pastor should focus upon getting to know the people and earning their respect. Respect for pastors comes when the congregation sees that you will show up for them in the hospital, at the funeral home when their loved ones pass on, and when you are at local events such as football games, basketball games, Lions Clubs, etc. But the respect also comes when you preach and teach sound doctrine.

"Many members of your congregation have been attending church since before you were born. They have a keen ear for what is right and what is wrong. They really have heard everything I've told you to do before – in fact, the real problem is that they've heard these ideas so many times that they won't focus upon it. When they look around, they see everyone else just sitting in the pews, so their worldly nature tells them to just compare themselves to the people around them.

"In many ways, this is what the problem in our churches is. Everyone considers that they will be a "regular" Christian and not a "fanatic". In other words, they will be lukewarm. But Jerry, what happens to meat when it sits at room temperature for a few days."

"Huh? It rots!"

"That's right! Meat rots at room temperature. For meat to be good for you, you need to kill the rot-causing bacteria with a hot temperature. And so, as the people gain respect for you, you'll need to begin to turn up the temperature – you'll need to convince them of three things.

"First, they need to understand that the Great Commission applies to every Christian, not just the pastors and Sunday school leaders. Everyone is called to speak the Gospel to others.

"Second, your flock needs to understand that almost everyone in the congregation is capable of leading people to Christ. Naturally, there are some people whose mental or physical handicaps are so extreme that they cannot lead people to Christ.

"Third, you'll need to kindle a fire in your people so that they will catch the vision and desire to lead people to Christ. And this three-step process takes time – about three years or so, in my experience.

"So, year one, teach the basics: Praise God to friends, neighbors, and family. Begin to move the congregation away from their most obvious country club ideas – you do know what a country club idea is, don't you?"

"I suspect you're going to tell me."

"A country club idea is the idea that the church is a club which takes care of the members first, second, and last. But we know now that the church is supposed to focus upon people outside the church, people who have just begun attending the church, and train the people who have been here the longest to be the best apostles that they can be."

"Interesting. I've never thought of a church as a country club, but I guess many churches do operate that way, with the pastor being the country club butler."

"That's right. You may need to break that country club idea to make good headway, otherwise people will begin to visit the church but will never feel accepted.

"Anyway, your second year, you can expect a couple of people to 'get it'. Support them in whatever outreach they try. Look to expand on what they start. For example, someone may want to start a kid's after-school program. Be there to help but let that someone lead the program. Back them up, brag on them Sunday mornings, and generally let everyone know that you're also looking for the second outreach program.

"The third year, you can expect the character of the church to start changing, because a bit of success goes a long way. Now, you can start putting 'wish lists" in the bulletin – ministry ideas and material donations that you'd like to see. Let people come to you to talk about those items that they feel passionate about.

"I will. And...thanks." Jerry really liked his friend. "When were you on Cyprus?"

A far-off look came into Larry's eyes. "A long, long time ago. I lost a good friend there...but I found my wife. "

Jerry let it drop. After some more discussion about Donna's progress, they went their separate ways.

Discussion and Thought Questions

1. What is the purpose of your church council?

2. What does your church council do?

3. What could your church council do to support the Mission?

4. What technology or worship style changes has your congregation considered? Why did you consider them?

Chapter Eleven - Some Details

It was a crisp, fall day, and Donna was walking home from work when she saw a familiar face – it was Larry.

"How're ya doin'?" he asked her.

"I'm doing great. But there are a couple of people I'm having trouble getting to church," she responded.

"Who ever said it was your job to get people to church?" Larry asked in an intense way.

"But…Isn't that the whole idea of the Great Commission?" Donna was confused.

"Nope. The whole idea of the Great Commission is to make disciples. Getting people into church is just one strategy for making disciples – and most people go about it backwards, anyway."

"What do you me?" Donna asked.

"Let me explain:" Larry responded.

"If you recall, the Great Commission of Matthew 18:16-20 tells us to lead people to baptism and teach them everything Christ has commanded. Now Paul later wrote that we are not to quit assembling together, and that is good advice. Christians need the help of other Christians to stay focused upon Christ.

"But getting people to church isn't the goal. It is a strategy that developed a long time ago but doesn't work well today. Let me ask you a question. Why don't people want to go to church?"

Donna thought a moment. "Well, some people say it's boring; others are afraid they'll be judged and looked down upon by the people there, still others say they don't have the time – Sunday morning is the only time they can sleep in – and some other people say it's because of soccer practice or work. There are a host of reasons, really."

"Those are all excuses, "Larry said, waving his arm for emphasis. "The real reason people don't come to church is because they aren't Christians."

"But I've got several Christian friends who don't come to church because they don't like the people there!" Donna was insistent.

"Now Donna, listen to me. There are a few Christians who can't make it to church because of health reasons, or because they don't have transportation. But people who are truly trying to follow Christ come to church. Those people you're talking about are probably people I call "ethnic" Christians."

"Ethnic Christians?"

"Yes. We have to recognize that there is a phenomenon that has developed in the church – it has always been there, actually, but it has become more obvious in the last fifty years. The Jewish people have recognized this for a long time in their communities. It is the person who self-identifies with the religion but doesn't observe the religion. And so, the Jews talk about 'observant' Jews who attend synagogue and 'ethnic' Jews, people who rarely, if ever, attend services. In the Christian community, we have the very same thing – ethnic Christians are people who claim to be Christian but do not show any signs of it to outsiders."

Larry continued. "You see, what happened was that Grandmother regularly went to church. Mother began skipping church in high school and only goes on Christmas Eve. Her grown children have almost never gone to church, so all they understand about Christianity is that it involves God and Jesus in some vague way. When you ask them, they tell you that they "believe in God" and never mention Christ. Since they know they aren't Moslem or Buddhist or Hindu or Jewish, then they believe in their own minds that they are Christian. But they aren't. At best, they have what George Barna calls a "mildly therapeutic theism". Theism is a belief in a god, and it makes them feel better. Thus, the "mildly therapeutic theism" label."

"But don't surveys tell us that 85% of the people in America are Christian?" Donna asked.

"Yes, that's what the surveys say. About 85% Christian, 3% Jewish, 2% Buddhist, 3% Moslem – and the rest are "nones", people who admit to no religious faith. But of those 85% Christian, only about 25-30% of them attend church once a month or more often. Let's assume that 5-10% can't attend because of illness or transportation or work schedules. That means that half the people in America claim to be Christian but don't come to church even once a month. These are your ethnic Christians. And we need to recognize that they aren't Christians."

"We'll, I always thought that becoming a Christian was simply a matter of declaring you were a Christian and believed in God," Donna pushed back.

"No, Daughter. That's similar to the way you become a Buddhist or a Moslem, but Christianity has always had a bit higher standard than that. Let's take it apart.

"Billy Graham told us repeatedly that becoming a Christian is a matter of 'believing in the Lord Jesus Christ.' That was a bit of shorthand, and today's preachers have often shortened it still more to 'believe in Jesus'. But the real aspects of salvation are a bit more complex.

"The first step, of course, is when God decides to bring a person into God's Kingdom. God's Holy Spirit sends people and events into the person's life which gently lead them to recognize their own inability to cope with the world. At that point, the person usually experiences a crisis – a time when they are forced to reevaluate the way they've looked at the Universe. When someone like you, Donna, explains to them the Good News of Jesus Christ, then they can choose to turn over control of their life to Jesus, and follow Him.

"Notice that this is not 'believing in God' but is instead a first step toward trusting God's Son, Jesus Christ, as a teacher, a leader, and the king of their lives. Part of why we trust Jesus is our understanding that Jesus is divine in some way we usually don't understand at this point, and so what is important is tying together in our mind three things: God exists. Jesus is God's Son. And following Jesus will get us out of trouble.

"Now some people have to go through that first step, getting clear in their mind that God exists. But our first step in salvation is when we recognize that Jesus Christ is worthy of being followed.

"This wasn't so important in the days when Christianity was the only religion most people had access to, but in today's world, when there are active mosques and synagogues and temples in every major city, it is important to help people clarify what makes Christianity unique and true.

Donna had been listening intently." Are you saying that 'belief in God' isn't enough?"

"That's exactly what I'm saying. A vague belief in the existence of a vague god gives you a vague religion. Instead, we need to be helping people understand that Christians consider Jesus Christ to be divine, God on this earth in the flesh, walking, talking, eating, breathing with us. Emanu-el. God with us. "

"Oh! That way they won't have all the confusion about whether or not Allah is the Christian God or not, "Donna jumped ahead.

"That's part of it, "Larry responded. "But the real point is that it helps people see that we have a concrete historicity to our faith, that our faith is not a matter of speculative opinion about who God is and what God wants. Our faith is grounded in what Jesus taught about the truths found in the Old Testament and what He taught that was new. Otherwise, you end up with a Design-Your-Own religion and a Design-Your-Own god. And that doesn't help anyone.

"Now there's a bit more to this salvation stuff. You and I both know that there are big arguments about baptism and whether or not it is necessary for your salvation. I'd like to look at this through a key question. What is salvation?"

Donna looked down. She thought for a minute. "I guess salvation is going to Heaven?" She seemed unsure of herself.

"That's only part of salvation. There are two aspects of salvation that are critical here. Most people look only at salvation from death and hellfire, or salvation from God's wrath, which is focused most surely upon those people who are in rebellion to God. In this view, God is like a king who has rebels in his territory. Simply by being in rebellion, they are lawbreakers guilty of the terrible crime of treason, which is a capital crime worthy of death. This is what Martin Luther called, 'the condition of sin'. Sin, you may know, comes from an old word which means "outside". And when Adam and Eve rebelled against God, all of their children were by birth rebels – what we call 'original sin' – born outside of God's kingdom."

Donna listened. "So, sinners are born to be rebels and are in rebellion to God."

"That's right. Everyone is born in rebellion, and acts in the most selfish ways possible. Look at infants – they care nothing for others – that has to be taught. Instead, they care only for their own comfort and will do anything to get their way."

"I never looked at it that way," Donna said. "Both my boys were pretty demanding when they were born."

"All children are demanding because they don't have the Holy Spirit. Anyone who hasn't received and listened to the Holy Spirit has an independent spirit and tries to be his or her own god, controlling everything in a bubble around them that constantly expands and damages everyone else near them. And those damaged people damage other people and children, and that's why our world is a mess – because we all went our own way.

"But when we realize that there is a better way and accept God's gift of salvation, declaring that we 'believe' or are now following Jesus, God declares us to be justified, which is a fancy word for "declared not guilty" of rebellion."

"But what about people who sin?" Donna asked. "I still sin even though I've followed Jesus for years."

"That is where Luther points out that in addition to the 'condition' of sin, - the state of rebellion to God - there are also 'acts' of sin – crimes we commit against God. Just as a rebel is likely to commit many crimes against the king and a loyal subject is less likely to commit those crimes, people who are in a state of sin are more likely to commit sin acts than people who are followers of Christ. In fact, as a former rebel becomes more and more aware of what his king wants, and becomes more and more loyal, he will commit less and less criminal acts. And so it is with the acts of sin. As people learn more and more about God's laws and love Jesus more and more, they commit less and less sin acts in their lives. We call this 'becoming holy' or sanctification."

"Okay! That makes sense now. I always wondered how that worked!" Donna was excited.

"Now there is the purpose of baptism. While some people say that baptism is nothing more than a public declaration that you are now following Jesus, Jesus never did anything which was essentially meaningless. Instead, while we are saved from God's wrath when we choose to follow Jesus, we still need to be saved from our own foolishness. In baptism, God reaches down into our hearts and makes an adjustment which allows us to now seek good. The Holy Spirit is prayed for and hands are laid onto the newly baptized. And now the Holy Spirit enters our heart and if we listen to the Spirit, we can be led into a life of truth and holiness. We can now be saved from our own foolishness."

"I just wish I could stop sinning," Donna said.

"Daughter, we all wish that. But that requires God's grace – God has to act upon us. But that is something we can all pray for, just like anything else. "

"What? Are you saying I can stop sinning?" Donna was incredulous.

Larry looked at her carefully. "God can do anything God wants. But God will not do anything to you which is essentially against your will. If you truly want to stop sinning, ask God to make you morally perfect, which means you only love God. God can do it. But the real problem is most people still have other loves, other idols, other wants which are stronger than their love for God. That is the task for the rest of your life – learning to love God more than anyone or anything else. This is what John Wesley called 'being made perfect in love'."

Donna looked down again. "I understand. I wish there was a shorter way."

Larry looked at her with compassion. "Look up Phoebe Palmer on the internet and read her book *"The Way of Holiness"*. You might be one of the rare ones who can take a shorter way."

Donna continued looking down for a while, thinking about what Larry had said.

"Donna, all this talk of salvation and ethnic Christians has a purpose. It's to help you understand one key point – people who aren't Christians don't want to come to church."

"I understand that – but that seems obvious."

"Well, it is obvious. It is so obvious that millions of Christians across the country overlook it. They spend all their time in 'outreach', trying to get non-Christians into church. But we know that people who are in rebellion to God will not have any interest in going to a place which is filled with loyal subjects of God, which is decorated to point people to God, and even smells like God is there. Yet what do people do? People 'invite people to church' and then get frustrated when these non-Christians don't show up.

"Instead, we have to remember – we have to help people become Christians before they will want to come to church. They must reach the point in their life where they are so interested in learning more about God and Jesus and what they have to offer that they will ask to come to your church. Otherwise, they will not be happy to be there – and we get frustrated with them. "

"So what should we do?" Donna looked hopeless. "Just give up?"

"No! We simply have to explain the Gospel to people with such love and clarity that they will want to commit their lives to following Christ even before they ever step in a church.

"You see, nothing fails like success. "

Donna raised a questioning eyebrow, but Larry continued.

"In the mid-twentieth century, Billy Graham was very successful with his so-called crusades. Billy and his friends would come into town, spend months organizing the local churches, praying, getting people to pray, training people, and then Billy would begin to preach. It was a big event – the newspapers and television stations were wall-to-wall Billy. They broadcast it on television for a hundred miles around. And when people went to hear Billy preach, many of the people took their friends that they had been talking to about Jesus to hear Billy, so Billy could make the Gospel clear to them. And it worked – about three percent of all the people who went to Billy Graham's crusades came forward to the altar calls."

"Three percent? Only three percent? I thought it was much more than that, "Donna said.

"Only three percent. Of course, that meant thousands of people each evening came forward, because Billy used stadiums that seated a hundred thousand people or more. And even more – there were the people who came to Jesus because of the television broadcasts. And all those people were connected with a local church for follow-up. It was a good, successful operation – but it doesn't work that way in the local church."

"Why not?" Donna wanted to know.

"Because on an average Sunday, there are very few people in a church who have not yet encountered Jesus, because non-Christians don't go to church." Larry moved his arm to chop at the last four words.

He continued. "That's why your pastor shouldn't preach like Billy Graham – evangelistic sermons are for crowds of mixed Christians and non-Christians. When the church doesn't have any non-Christians present, the preacher needs to focus on building up the skills and holiness of the people, the Body of Christ – so they can explain the Gospel to people one-on-one in the coffee shops and McDonalds and living rooms and kitchens of the world. Save the evangelistic sermons for Christmas and Easter and early September when people are trying out church again.

"The basic skill you need, now that you've learned how to praise God to your neighbors, friends, and family, is to explain the Gospel. And the best way to explain the Gospel is to listen to people – I mean really listen to them, especially as they tell their tales of trouble and woe. After you've listened to them for an hour and they've begun to run down, tell them 'I had a similar problem – not as bad, but similar' and then you tell them what God and Jesus did for you that day. Tell the truth – don't make it fancier than it was but tell your friend what you saw and experienced and heard and felt. And then tell them, "I know that Jesus could do something similar for you."

"Now after you've told that story, they'll tell you why things are different, why things are so much worse, why God wouldn't care about them – and then you tell them what God has promised: If you will turn around, look toward Jesus instead of the world for answers, God will forgive you of all your sins and crimes against God, and will accept you as God's adopted child with love. You might help them pray to God for forgiveness and to declare their intention to follow Jesus right then and there.

"Now, you have a new Christian. And very soon, as you continue to meet with him or her, they will be ready to come to church with you. So remember – the reason people don't come to church is because they aren't Christians, so we need to help them become Christians before they'll come to church. Amen?" Larry looked up at Donna.

"Amen, Larry. I'll try it." Donna paused. "Larry, there's something I think you should know. Pastor Jerry seems to be overwhelmed some days – I think he's working too many hours."

"I'll look into it." Larry assured her.

And they went their separate ways.

Discussion and Thought Questions

1. Why do you think people don't attend church?

2. Have you met any "ethnic Christians"?

3. How did your salvation come about?

4. Do you work on becoming more holy? How?

Chapter Twelve - Spending Time

Jerry was happy. As the bright leaves of fall filled the trees, the church had recovered, and now each Sunday there were about 30-35 people attending, and often 1 or 2 new people. Jerry was spending more and more time visiting with the people, both in their homes and at the hospital.

But there was a problem. He no longer had time to read theology, and he enjoyed reading theology. And so he was very happy when he saw a familiar face standing on the corner, waiting for him.

"Hello, Larry! I was just thinking about you." Jerry walked up and shook Larry's hand.

"Hello, Pastor! How are things going?"

Jerry told him about his time issues. "I just don't have enough time to do everything I think I need to do."

Larry thought a moment. "We've talked about the basic purpose of a church, which is fulfilling the Great Commission."

"Uh-huh. We are to make disciples who can make disciples, "Jerry responded.

"Okay, Jerry. What do you think your part in that is?" Larry looked at him with that intense look he so often had.

"Well, I used to think that my purpose was to bring people to the Lord, but now I'm not so sure. I just don't seem to have time."

Larry nodded. "You're right. Bringing people to the Lord is your purpose. But there is more to it than that. Let me explain.

"Jerry, a pastor is special in the church. It's not because you are particularly holy or anything like that – although, as you spend more time with God and the Holy Spirit and the Word, you will naturally become more holy than the average person. No, pastors are special because you've decided to become a professional Gospel-bringer. Your church is filled with amateurs, with volunteers, with people who are struggling to minister to other people while they live in this world and have other responsibilities. But you have decided to become a professional at this. And that makes you special – and gives you a special role.

"Your special role is to lead. Now Jesus had a lot to say to His disciples about the type of leadership He wanted, and it wasn't the leadership that we find in the world. So, we need to take a moment and understand where most people get their concepts of leadership."

"I got mine from my high school coach, Mr. Johnson, "Jerry interjected.

"That's good. Most people get their ideas of leadership from one of three sources – the military, their workplace, or their elementary teachers. Each of those sources shows us a different type of leader. For example, the army has the drill sergeant, the workplace has the supervisor or manager, and the school has the classroom teacher. Each is a leader – but none of them normally portrays the type of leadership that a church needs."

"Is that because they aren't spiritual?" Jerry wanted to know.

"Yes, but we need to recognize that there are some serious differences between churches and those other organizations. Let's look at the most basic. What happens when a man or woman decides to disobey their sergeant and walks out of the room?"

"They either go to Leavenworth prison, get discharged dishonorably, or get punished severely." Jerry laughed.

"And what happens in the workplace if people disobey the boss?"

"They get fired and lose their paychecks."

"And what about the school? What happens to students that disobey teachers?"

"Detention or a trip to the principal's office."

Larry looked Jerry in the eyes. "And what happens in a church if someone disobeys the pastor?"

Jerry sat there a minute. "I suppose nothing except they cause trouble in the body. You can't fire them or punish them."

"That's right. You see, you can't really punish people in the church because they can go right down the street to the next church and probably take a dozen people with them. You have no threat of paycheck or freedom or detention to hold over them. They can walk out anytime they want. The people of the church are there because they want to be there. Even the threat of excommunication used by the Catholic Church depends upon the person believing that their soul's situation in eternity depends upon being in good standing in the Catholic Church. For some people this is critical, but many other people simply leave the Church. And that changes the leadership dynamics completely.

"Perhaps the only outside people who really understand leadership the way it should be in a church are high school coaches and the leadership of highly creative companies, who look upon their top people as assets instead of costs."

"You mean companies like Apple and Google and Microsoft and advertising agencies?" Jerry was warming up to the idea.

"That's right! And so, Jesus talked about servant leadership – being a servant to the people you lead rather than ordering them around. And there's more to it than that.

"When a leader decides to be a servant, it means that his job – your job, Pastor – is to help those other people achieve great things. It is your job to provide them with training, with positive motivation, to help them use the power of the Holy Spirit, to let them run with the ideas that the Holy Spirit gives them. In effect, you must help them find out what the Holy Spirit wants them to do and then become or organize their support staff, letting them control their own ministries while you sit back and say, 'What can I do to help you?'" Larry was on a roll.

"That's different. I always thought I was supposed to do ministry." Jerry said.

"It is different from most churches. Your job is to equip *other* people to do ministry, helping them succeed beyond anything you could ever have done.

"There is another aspect to this. In most of our cities and towns, we learned our organizational models from old industry, who learned it from the military in World War II. A few brains and leaders at the top controlled many machines at the bottom, and those machines were tended by a costly group of workers. All the thinking happened at the top, and the average worker was asked to just do his or her dull job, attend work every day, be quiet, and go home. All the decisions were made by a few people at the top, and the profits were sent out of town to headquarters.

"And so, in the 1950's, our churches developed that way. A couple of staff and volunteer leaders made all the decisions for the church, and the rest of the people were expected to attend weekly, put money in the plate, listen quietly, and go home. Each church was expected to send money to a central headquarters, where the really 'important' people would see that it got used properly in foreign missions or wherever.

"But in our modern creative companies, they use servant leadership concepts. Now, each person is expected to use his or her brain to come up with ideas that improve their own area, and so instead of having 3 or 4 thinking people in a factory, the best companies have hundreds of people improving things, developing new products, and fixing production problems. The job of the people at the top is to help all those brains work better and achieve more things and be happier.

"In the same way, the best, fastest growing churches have figured out that the Great Commission applies to everyone, that the Holy Spirit can speak to anyone, that each person has a unique group of people whom they can reach through a unique ministry, and the job of the Pastor and staff of a church is to help people come to God through Christ, then help them to find their own ministry through the Word and the Holy Spirit, and teach people to listen to the Word and the Holy Spirit, becoming fully productive members of the Body of Christ." Larry finally stopped for a breath.

Jerry jumped in." So, you're saying I should be helping my people grow. How do I do that?"

"You'll need to pray for each person as you can and help each one individually. You are right – developing people for the Lord is your job. And that means that your best uses of time are generally the following:

"First, be sure that there is a great sermon each week. It doesn't have to be given by you, though. Other people can preach and should be given practice. A second service is a good idea, if only because it gives other people than you a chance to practice preaching. Make sure those sermons teach people something, move their hearts to love God and Christ, and lead people into truly worshipping the Trinity. People will praise God to their friends, neighbors, and family if you ask them, but they won't really develop the hearts to listen to messy people and lead them to Christ until they begin to love Him and the Father. So your sermons need to teach concrete ideas and help people love and worship the Trinity.

"Second, organize classes or groups that move people along the path of spiritual growth – and spiritual growth has several aspects. It combines understanding the Bible, understanding God, loving God, becoming committed to following Christ, and becoming holy people.

"You might have a confirmation or new person's class, a Christian Basics class which teaches basic Christian ideas, a more advanced spiritual disciplines class which teaches prayer, Bible study, and similar topics, an evangelism and apologetics course which turns disciples into apostles, and a leadership group which teaches other people how to lead in a church setting. Plus, you should always have a more traditional Bible study going on that uses the Bible as the textbook, working through various books of the Bible one at a time.

"Now, your church may be too small for all of these, but you can rotate these courses over a couple of years. Remember the stages of the people in your congregation. Some need to be led to a profession of faith and baptism, others need to be changed from merely attending to becoming regular disciples, others need to move onto apostleship, and still others into leadership. And all the people need to understand the Word of God more fully.

"But if I teach 4 or 5 classes a week and prepare a sermon, how will I ever get to visit people and do ministry?" Jerry wondered.

"You won't be able to. That is a part of your job you'll need to cut back on or even give up if you really want your church to grow. Instead, you need to teach several other people how to visit people in the hospital, how to visit new people, how to take communion to those at home, even how to be with the dying. Over time, as a church leader, you need to become more of a trainer of people and less a doer of care-giving ministry. Let me give you another idea about this.

"Let's assume that you try to visit two homes a day, which is realistically about the most a person can do consistently. That takes about 3 hours. That means that you can visit 60 homes every month, right?"

Jerry never was good at math, but that made sense to him. "Yes."

"Now, that means that if you average 2 people per home, you can keep visiting everyone in a 120-member church every month, and you spend about 7 x 3 hours, or 21 hours a week on this. But you need to do a sermon, and the difference between a sermon and a great sermon, most pastors have found, is the difference between spending 4 hours and spending 30 hours in the creation of the sermon, the illustrations, deciding upon the music, deciding upon supporting images for multimedia, and anything else you put in. So now you're spending 50 hours, and I haven't even begun to look at class preparation, funerals, weddings, board meetings, finance committees, and the time you actually spend teaching or preaching."

"I see…there just isn't enough time, is there?"

"No. You have to recognize that there are some things that take a set amount of time, no matter how big the congregation, and other things that require more time the bigger the congregation grows. For example, developing a great sermon takes 30 hours a week, no matter the size of the congregation or how many times it will be delivered. Preparing a great musical piece takes a certain amount of practice whether there are 10 people in the audience – or 500 people. Teaching a class requires an hour for the class and a few hours to prepare, no matter how many people are in the class.

"But visiting everyone in the hospital takes an hour a person – or 10 minutes per person if you just 'greet, pray, and retreat' – whether there is 1 person in the hospital or 25 people in the hospital. And counseling people one-on-one requires an hour per person. And so, as your congregation grows, you will need to focus upon what is critical – and let those items whose time commitment grows with the size of the congregation be delegated to other people you have trained to do their part.

"In 1981, Eugene Peterson wrote a deep, thoughtful piece for *Leadership Journal,* called "The Unbusy Pastor", in which he talked about his recognition that pastoral leaders need to intentionally plan time to be alone with God in prayer, with God's Word in study, and with the Holy Spirit in reflection, and even with other people in listening. This only happens when you realize what is truly important for a pastor – leading the church, understanding God's will for yourself and your church, and learning to listen to the Holy Spirit and the Word of God.

"One of the greatest problems in many churches is that the church committee deems its role to be 'managing ministry'. The committee spends the meeting time telling the pastor and staff what to do. This can become a source of great frustration between the pastor and the people on the committee. But at good churches, the committees are actually teams. They 'do ministry' instead of 'manage ministry'. This is why the Trustees committee at most churches actually works well – the Trustees recognize that they are the repair and construction people for the church, fixing the plumbing, painting the walls, repairing the broken windows. You see, they usually act as a ministry team instead of a ministry-managing committee. In a good church, most of the committees operate as teams. For example, a 'worship committee' might tell the pastor what they want to see in worship, while a 'worship team' actually gets involved in the weekly worship, selecting and performing the music, reading the scripture, decorating the sanctuary, purchasing or making banners, setting up candles – you get the picture. People get involved this way.

"Jerry, what does your denomination say that only you can do?"

Jerry pondered a few seconds. "I'm the only one authorized to bless communion, to baptize, and to perform marriages. Everything else I can delegate – even preaching and performing funerals…Wow! That's a lot of things that I could hand off!...But what would people say?"

"That, my young friend, is the problem. Peterson suggests that you put time in your appointment calendar to read, to pray, to study, to work on sermons…even to go out with your wife if you have one…and then tell people that you can't visit or do something because you already have an appointment at that time." Larry smiled. "By the way, do you have a girlfriend?"

"No, Larry. I haven't had time to look for one, either…OH! That's part of the reason I need to delegate, isn't it?"

"Yes. A wife is a wonderful thing to have. A God-fearing wife who is also called to ministry can make the difference between a good pastor and a great pastor. Finding her is well worth the time and effort." Larry's eyes seemed to be looking at a daydream.

"Larry, are you okay?"

"Yes. Just remembering…Well, Pastor, I've got to run. I'm picking up someone at the airport and I need to hit the road. See you soon!"

And with that, Larry walked down the street and around the corner.

Discussion and Thought Questions

1. What do you think your pastor spends time doing each week? Roughly how much time does your pastor spend on each item?

2. Ask your pastor to explain a normal week – and a busy week to you.

3. What items should your pastor begin to delegate? What items are you willing to learn how to do?

4. How many people – and specifically which people – spend significant time doing church business other than Sunday mornings?

5. Which of your church committees operate as 'ministry-management' committees, and which operate as 'ministry teams'?

Chapter Thirteen - The Airport

As Larry drove to the Port Columbus airport, his mind wandered. He was thinking of when he had first met his wife.

...

The Middle Eastern port was filled with people, the smell of grilled lamb was in the air. He was waiting dockside, when they arrived – his friends, and a young, dark-haired beauty. She smiled at him as he helped her onto the plank that ran to the small boat.

...

Time to exit from I-70 north onto I-670. Some rain was beginning to fall, something that was much rarer and exciting in his hometown, but here it meant there would soon be a traffic jam. He hoped he wouldn't be late – he still had plenty of time.

The Columbus, Ohio area was where he was working now. Others were working in India and Indonesia, in Pakistan and Nigeria. His wife was due in from China. But he had been led to work in Ohio because, with its high tech industry and wealth, with its many colleges and universities, it was balanced between becoming a Christian center which would lead the nation and becoming a center of atheism and Islam – the late-coming religion had significant outposts in Detroit and Toledo, which were beginning to move into Columbus. The only good way to counterbalance the greater family size of the Moslems was to train some excellent Christian leaders, leaders who could return Christianity from the moral system the Americans had made it to the complete life-system and explanation of the Universe that it was meant to be by Y'shua.

He thought back to the early days of Christianity, when people were excited and transformed by the knowledge that God had visited earth again, that God had declared love for all people, that God's Son had died to bring everyone who followed Him eternal life. Larry thought of the excitement of the time, the wonderful days expressed in Acts chapter 2, the rapid growth of the Way, and also how those flaming fires had died down to smoldering embers in America. He thought of how so many church leaders were committed to keeping their church's door open, when their calling was to be so much more. For Larry knew that any pastor was called to not only be priest, business manager, and counselor, but also was called to be a prophet, potentially capable of doing the great deeds of Elijah, of Elisha who was even greater, of Nathan, of Moses, of Joshua, of Jeremiah, of Isaiah. Yet so many pastors thought of themselves as having no ability to affect the world. And, of course, the reason was that they did not truly believe that the Holy Spirit could speak to and work through them.

And that was his mission – strengthening promising pastors wherever the Spirit led him. And the way Larry did this was ultimately to help those pastors listen to the Holy Spirit.

The rain on the highway and the wet, glistening leaves on the trees beside the road reminded him of Massachusetts…

…

The 25-year old boy was dressed in black as a good pastor should be. Larry hailed him …" Reverend Edwards! Reverend Edwards! "

The young pastor stopped and turned. "How may I help you, sir?" In the boy's eyes flashed intense intelligence and Larry could feel the Holy Spirit in the young man.

"I have just come from Connecticut, from Yale, and the men there spoke highly of you. May I impose upon your time and discuss some theological matters with you?" Larry was formal, as was the custom in this society.

"I'm headed toward prayers at this moment, but if you would like to come around to the parsonage around dark, I could devote the evening to you."

Larry bowed. "That would be excellent. Thank you, sir."

…

Larry turned off on the airport exit and drove to the short-term parking. He checked his watch. Good. Still 15 minutes until her plane landed.

The chill of the damp October evening hit him as he opened the car door and walked through the parking garage. He saw movement ahead in the shadows. The Spirit shouted at him – "GO DOWNSTAIRS!" and he quickly went down the stairs. It was just like that night in Germany…

…

In the dream, all was pleasant. Suddenly, Y'shua came before him and said, "You must arise and leave this country for America at once." And then he woke up. Without question, Larry packed a bag, walked to the railway station, and took a train headed to Paris, arriving around noon. Late that evening, the word came over the radio of the Kristallnacht, the night of broken glass when the persecution of the Jews began.

As he entered the terminal, he heard a shot and a shout from behind him on the floor where his car was parked. Security guards and police began running past him. "Thank you, Lord, once again!" he said thankfully. A woman looked at him strangely as she overheard him.

The Holy Spirit often spoke to Larry, and over a long lifetime, Larry had learned to listen to the Spirit. Rarely loud, the Spirit was a still, small voice on the edge of his mental consciousness, gentling guiding him one way or the other. It had saved his life several times, and the Spirit's guidance had led him to participate in wonderful things of God. And so, he kept one part of his mind always on the listen for that still, small voice.

Looking at the screens, he found that his wife's plane was right on time. So he moved to baggage claim and took a seat. He enjoyed sitting in airports, there were so many people to watch and to speak to.

Soon, a young woman with a sleeping infant sat down two seats away. The Spirit said to Larry, "Speak!" So, Larry spoke to the woman.

"Waiting for his father?" he hazarded a guess.

"Yes. His dad is coming home from Korea." The woman was holding back tears.

"Ma-am… are you okay?" Larry leaned toward her.

"Well, it just that I found out this week that Bobby has leukemia, and Robert doesn't know yet. I'm so scared about Bobby. "The tears began to flow.

Larry looked at her carefully. She had no obvious signs of the Faith. "I'm a pastor. Where do you attend church?"

"We don't. "

"What part of town do you live in?"

"We live in Mount Carmel, east of the city."

"You do? We'll that's great. The Lord has been working already. You see, I have a good friend who is the pastor at Mount Carmel Church. He's a great young man…and I know that he can help you and your husband through these difficult times."

"But how can he help?"

"Ma-am, Jesus raised people from the dead. He can surely help a child with leukemia. And if you ask Him, Jesus will be with you through the entire ordeal. And I might be able to give you some ideas about how to tell your husband about Bobby's leukemia."

They talked another 20 minutes, she cried much of the time, and eventually they prayed together.

And just as she said, "Amen", a short, dark, athletic woman apparently in her 40's walked up.

"Tabby!" Larry stood up.

"Larry!" They hugged.

"Suzy, I'd like you to meet my wife, Tabby. Tabby, Suzy Long and her son Bobby. Suzy just told me that her son has been diagnosed with leukemia. They're waiting on Robert, her husband, who was flying in from Korea where he's in the Army."

"Oh, let me hold him…Robert. He was upgraded to first class and sat beside me all the way in. But he didn't seem upset or anything."

"He doesn't know yet." Larry said, quietly, as a large, handsome young man in uniform walked up.

"Suzy!" Robert picked her up.

Suzy mouthed "Thank you" to Larry as she was whirled around.

The five of them exchanged introductions – Larry had already given Suzy his card and Jerry's phone number – and then Larry and Tabby walked away.

"How was Shanghai?" he asked her.

"Yo Ling is now meeting with ten girls at her apartment each week. And two of the girls will be able to lead their own groups when they split up next month."

"Next month? I thought they could grow to 30 people?"

"Legally, they can, but I'd like to keep them below the radar. So I've suggested that they hold to a fifteen person maximum, then split into three groups. Those Chinese laws on assembly grow leaders quickly, don't they?"

"They sure do. Sometimes I wish the entire world limited our church sizes. Then, people would have to grow and participate." Larry was thoughtful. "But there are other advantages to the mega-churches."

Larry navigated her around the police presence on the third floor. "What happened?" Tabby asked.

"There was a shooting. As usual, the Spirit warned me when I arrived."

"Larry, that's four incidents this year for you. You must have something really big brewing."

"I feel I do. It may not look like it. But I feel I do."

They kissed as he opened the car door for her.

As they drove out, Tabby asked, "How are things going here?"

"I've been working with a promising pair – a young man and a young woman. Now, the Spirit says I've got to bring them together. I guess a good couple can accomplish a lot for the Lord, "Larry grinned over at his wife as he accelerated onto the Interstate.

She smiled back at the love of her life.

And the rest of their evening is none of our business.

Discussion and Thought Questions

1. What has been your experience of the Holy Spirit?

2. Has the Holy Spirit ever guided you the way it guided Larry?

3. How does the Holy Spirit speak to you?

4. How do you react to the Holy Spirit?

5. Are you open to meeting people in public spaces? Give an example of a situation where you met someone and talked about God with them.

6. Have you considered how a marriage can become a partnership for spreading the Gospel?

Chapter Fourteen - A Pair of Diners

Jerry and Sarah arrived at Fred's Diner at the same time. They recognized each other from ecumenical training meetings. "What are you doing over here?" Jerry asked.

"A guy who is mentoring me invited me, "was her low-key response.

"That's funny – I'm meeting my mentor, too," Jerry replied.

At about this time, Larry walked in. "Shall the three of us sit together?"

The two pastors looked at each other and nodded. "Sure, "Sarah said.

A brisk young woman with the name "Ramona" on an engraved nametag led them to their booth. Handing them menus, she took their drink order and left them.

"I bet you're wondering why I brought the two of you here today at the same time." Larry began and watched their heads nod. "There are two reasons.

"First, you two need to become friends, because you're both in the same business and working near each other. It always helps to have someone to lift you up who is not of your congregation, and not in your chain of command.

"Second, as you have guessed by now, my time is limited and you both need to hear the same advice this time."

Jerry looked at Sarah, then turned back to Larry. "What's that?"

About this time Ramona stopped by and took their orders. Jerry ordered a cheeseburger and fries, Sarah ordered a salad, and Larry had a fish sandwich.

After Ramona left, Larry began to speak.

"You've both begun to make appropriate changes in how you are leading your churches, and you both understand the purpose of the church. Now, I'm going to give you some background and theory so you can take things to the next level, ok?"

Sarah nodded for both of them. "Sure!"

Larry continued. "Over the centuries, different churches have developed different paradigms of doing church. Different ways and methods. For example, in the Middle Ages, the Catholic Church had the paradigm which said that the church was a civic function, that the priest performed the Mass, his homilies helped the people remember that God was in charge, and that continued attendance at the Mass was necessary to keep your immortal soul from spending eternity in Hell. In essence, the purpose of the medieval Church was partially to keep people from Hell and partially to ensure a reasonably law-abiding population in the town. The priest provided sacraments almost as a public service. Just as the grocer provided food to keep the body alive, the Church provided the sacraments to keep the soul alive. I simplify, of course, and mean no disrespect to the Catholic Church.

"During this time, the laity did very little unless they were wealthy, for the average person was illiterate, destitute, and busy trying to survive. Wealthier men and women supported the church and their younger sons usually became the next generation of priests.

"Towards the end of the Middle Ages, some of the leaders in Rome began to look upon the local churches as a revenue source, especially as the Popes became increasingly involved in secular politics and the Papal States controlled large sections of central Italy.

"Then, as the Reformation came around, the purpose of the Church began to vary because different branches of the Reformation developed different paradigms for doing church.

"For example, the Anabaptists – the Mennonites and Amish – felt that the Christian faith was best lived in community, and the central church meeting took on aspects of a town meeting or extended family reunion. The leaders of the church became the leaders of the community, a community that was joined by a common desire to do God's will in a particular pattern of life.

"On the other hand, the Calvinists and their British cousins, the Puritans, looked upon the church as a way to instruct people in behavior, as a means for controlling the wilder elements of the community through the understanding of God's laws and commands, as well as a way to Heaven.

"As the church moved to America and America matured, several other paradigms came into being while many of the old paradigms continued. By the late 20th century and early 21st century, most churches fell into one of several styles, all the while giving an outward statement that they exist to worship God:

"To some, the local church is a fund-raising community for social ministries and missionary organizations. And so, much of the instruction from the central command structure of the denomination is oriented toward ensuring a strong revenue flow from the local churches to central coffers, and then the money is distributed to these social ministries and missionaries.

"To others, the local church is a local platform for social ministries. These churches are the churches you hear about that have the food pantries, the soup kitchens, the clothes closets, and similar ministries. Their people are actively involved in these organizations.

"Many dying churches exist as a social club, or country club. They see their purpose is to listen to God's word together – but their actual primary purpose is to support themselves, to take care of the various members, and to provide a sense of belonging for each other. Stronger versions of these churches actually act as networking centers for the professionals in their towns.

"Other churches see themselves as fishing boats or lighthouses, rescuing sinners from the waters of despair, pulling them into their lifeboats, and applying spiritual first aid to help them survive in society.

"Still other churches, rare as they are, see themselves as a training ground or college. Their purpose is to bring people into the body, to train people up in the body, and to forward them back into the world as mission leaders, ready to start new churches, new ministries, or lead existing churches and ministries.

"And so we come to the question of the day. What is the paradigm that your church follows? The answer is critical because it determines what will happen to your church."

"What do you mean?" Sarah asked.

"Well, if your church sees itself as a platform for social ministries, you will see much activity as long as you have people with the age and energy to work in those ministries. You will be attractive to young professionals who want something productive to do in their leisure time. Then, as your church population ages, your church's ability to operate these ministries will decline unless you can bring new workers into the ministries themselves.

"On the other hand, if your church sees itself as a fund-raising church for outside or central missions, then your church will do well as long as you have professionals and wealthy retirees in the church. But you won't be very attractive to younger people who are financially struggling.

"If your church sees itself as a lifeboat, it may grow tremendously, but will eventually need to develop a training program for internal leadership.

"So what is the paradigm that your church follows?"

Jerry thought for a moment. "When I first met you, you pointed out that the mission of the church was given by Jesus in the Great Commission of Matthew 28:16-20. But now, are you saying that the church can act as a social service ministry platform instead."

Larry responded quickly. "No! But I'm saying that many churches in our world have chosen that paradigm of operation. It is possible to operate as a social services ministry platform. But there are issues that develop in a church that chooses to do that. First and foremost is the problem that social services, which could be a *strategy* for the goal of spreading the Gospel and bringing people into the Kingdom, becomes instead the *goal* of the strategies of the church. I've seen this happen time and time again. The cart moves in front of the horse.

"Unless the pastor is constantly preaching about the Great Commission, unless the pastor is constantly teaching people to speak the Good News to people, unless the pastor is constantly active in this manner, the members of the congregation will forget their mission and begin to believe that their mission is simply to provide food or clothing or utility help to the poor, when it could be much more than that – it could be the salvation of people's eternal souls with the church using the contacts made by the food pantry or the soup kitchen or the clothes closet as the first step in spreading the Gospel to people.

"Here's a quick test to see if your church is following the Great Commission or is locked in the social services deathtrap – visit the key ministry or ministries while they are in operation. Observe. Are the people who are doing the ministry work taking time to pray with almost every person? Are they working with them spiritually? Are they teaching scriptural lessons? Or are they just concerned with efficiently getting people food or clothing or helping them pay their bills?

"If your church is focused upon being a fund-raising organization, it is very difficult for them to be following the Great Commission, because they may be operating with no personal contact with people outside the church. This paradigm was a legitimate paradigm when more than 90 percent of the people in America attended a church and claimed to be Christian, but it doesn't make sense today when over half the people in America do not attend church.

"So what is your paradigm?" Larry asked again.

Sarah answered this time. "I'm afraid we are the social services platform church. I've already noticed that the people working the food pantry aren't interested in talking to the people they serve – just in getting the orders filled. So what should I do?"

Larry answered. "First of all, you'll need to address the issue a few times from the pulpit. I always follow the strategy that your congregation must be taught the biblical principles first before you get specific about the application in ministry. So, I would begin preaching about the need to connect with people in general, the need to speak the words of the Gospel to people as well as 'showing the Gospel in our lives' in several sermons first. Then, I would begin to get specific after I gave them a few weeks to grasp the concept that they should actually talk to people about Christ. By getting specific, I'd begin to preach about combining action and speech whenever we help people. And only after preaching about these things a few times would I actually talk to the food pantry people about the issue. But even then, I would expect that there are people who will push back, wanting to work efficiently rather than work spiritually."

Jerry asked, "What do you mean by working spiritually?"

Larry continued, "In every group of people, there are essentially two types of people. There are task-oriented people who want to get the job done quickly, efficiently, and effectively. There are also people-oriented people who are more concerned with talking, with understanding how the grandkids and nephew are, how Bill's cancer treatment is going, and generally lubricating the social wheels of the group. The people-oriented people drive the task-oriented people crazy because the task-oriented people want to get the work done and all those other people want to do is talk, while the task-oriented people drive the people-oriented people crazy by being pushy and rushing everyone.

"In a company, the people-oriented people naturally gravitate towards sales and customer service, while the task-oriented people move toward production, design, and back office work. But in a church, these people end up working together on the same teams. And this can cause trouble, particularly when a leader is strongly task- or people-oriented.

"And so the thing we have to remember is that in a church, the task *is* the people. People development is the task we are trying to accomplish with God's direct involvement. That's what I mean by working spiritually. We work and we talk, but the talk is about spiritual matters and how spiritual lessons can solve practical problems.

"Everything we do needs to be looked at through that lens – will this project, this event, this procedure help people grow closer to Christ? Yes, we need to be reasonably efficient, but we will never match a restaurant in our dining experience, we will never match professional musicians in our musical performance, and we will never even match a government agency in the efficiency of our social services. For there is a difference – we are a church, and a church is focused upon people's eternal souls much more than their dining experiences, their entertainment, or their financial needs.

"And so we spend a bit longer time in rehearsals talking, because the musicians love each other, and we stumble across each other in the kitchen and always have Sally's horrible cake because we love Sally and know that that is the way she gives back to the church, and we take three times as long to fill that food pantry order because we sit and listen and pray with the people who come in. That's what it means to be a church, and that's what it means to work spiritually.

"You know, so many times we get hung up because we develop a training or a Bible study and people want to go down rabbit trails, talking about issues that aren't in our lesson plan. Learn to accept those and let those rabbits run until they really go off in the weeds, because those small groups are great times to help people firm up their faith. For example, you might have a lesson to cover Acts Chapter 2, but one question leads to another and the real discussions becomes the pre-incarnate Christ. That's ok – let the discussion run.

"Now if the discussion starts moving into gossip or unproductive church politics, then I will 'shoot the rabbit' and put us back on track. And so, when you expect 10 people at a Bible Study class and only 2 people show up, be glad since you get to develop those 2 people faster because they will feel free to ask the questions that are truly important to them. That's what it means to develop people. I once led a church with about 120 people in regular worship – and 12 of them became district trained ministry leaders. You can never have too many Christian leaders or leaders that are too well trained."

Sarah and Jerry were sitting with open mouths.

"You two look like you've never heard this before."

Jerry started. "I haven't, and it puts a new spin on things. But don't you have to be careful who you select as leaders?"

"Not really. That's the business of the Holy Spirit. Oh, you want to be sure that they are believers and not followers of a different religion, and you'd like to make sure they don't have any public, obvious, blatant sin – you wouldn't move a person accused of adultery who is in the midst of a messy divorce into leadership. You'd wait a couple of years and see how things shake out. You might also avoid putting a highly abrasive, angry person in leadership. But don't spend a lot of time looking for "the best", because you have no way of knowing who the Holy Spirit will make into the next Billy Graham. Instead, look for people hungry to grow and make a difference.

"You see, in industry, most companies believe that a leader is a rare and expensive thing, and since leaders must be paid more than regular employees, most companies are very careful to only select a handful of leaders.

"But in the best companies today, the management has recognized that people who are in management and trained well are more devoted to the company, think more about solving company problems, and generally are much more productive than untrained, ordinary employees, and so they do crazy things to get more managers. At one company I know, they like to give a new manager who was only a year or two out of college one or two new employees to manage while the 'manager' continues to spend most of his or her time working on the project directly. The reason is that the 'manager' is now more committed to solving the company problems.

"It's the same in churches – except that since most people are volunteers, it doesn't really cost anything to have everyone trained as a Christian leader. We don't pay them a higher salary and so it doesn't cost us. Jesus showed us the example – He picked a rather motley crew to be in His core leadership team – Peter, Andrew, James, and John were all fishermen, and only Peter had any sort of leadership position on the boats. Simon the Zealot was a would-be terrorist. Matthew was a tax collector who operated on commission and was as popular as an IRS man at a Wall Street convention. It was much the same with the others – no one would have said, 'There will be your best disciple!' Yet they all ended up being heavily committed to the faith, all except Judas Iscariot.

"You see, the more someone feels like a leader in their church, the more they'll give in time, treasure and talents. They'll be more likely to evangelize and more likely to be positive about the church – if you give them the opportunity to use their time and talents.

"The best churches are continually urging people to step up to more and better training, to grow, to look at themselves as the leader of a small group, most of whom are people who don't even attend church, and they help everyone grow as fast as they want. That's how a church really grows – letting people run with what the Holy Spirit has gifted them with and led them to do. Churches die when people are held back."

Sarah jumped in. "I've seen that happen. When the praise band got started, I noticed that those musicians were there every week and almost never missed. Before, when all we had was the choir, they only attended every couple of weeks."

Larry came back, "That's right. Give people a chance to use their Spirit-given gifts and you'll be amazed at what they'll do for the Lord – and the church."

"Now, I have to run, so you two go ahead and finish eating. I've got the check." Larry paid for the check, and the two single pastors stayed for another hour, talking first of all about their ministry, and then increasingly about each other…

Discussion and Thought Questions

1. What process does your church use to select leaders?

2. Where you worked, how did management select leaders?

3. Are you more task-oriented, or more people-oriented?

4. Speak of a time when task-oriented people and people-oriented people irritated each other in your church.

5. What paradigm has your church followed?

Chapter Fifteen – The Last Visit

Larry awoke in his hotel room. "Time to move on," the Spirit said. "One last visit."

He got up from his bed, took a shower, and then packed up his suitcase. He wondered why the Spirit had sent him to this small town east of Columbus, but the Spirit always knew. Traveling all these years, Larry had become used to living out of a suitcase, but he still looked forward to his retirement home, that mansion prepared by Y'shua somewhere in New Jerusalem.

Before Larry left the room, he took out his Bible. In Greek, he read from John 11 – the chapter that always brought him to his knees in tears. But time had passed, and he would see them again one day.

Gopal Patel, the young man who had checked him in at the hotel during his first visit, was working that morning. Gopal greeted Larry with a huge smile. "Leaving us again?" he asked.

"Yes, but I fear this is my last visit here for a long time. How's the church working out for you?"

"I've made several new friends. And I'm in a study of Romans. I never realized how deep Christian philosophy could be. I want to thank you again for leading me to understand Christ." The young man practically bowed.

"You are a smart and wise man. It was a great pleasure to help you. I expect you to do great things for the Lord." Larry was sincere. The young man was sharp as a tack and took his newfound faith seriously. "Send me an email when you are ready to go to seminary. I'll write you a letter of recommendation."

"You are too kind! Thank you, sir! Will you pray with me once more before you go?"

"Of course." Larry prayed for the man and his future, took his receipt, and began to walk out to his car, when he suddenly stopped and looked at the headline on the local newspaper. "New 5,000 Home Development Planned for Mount Carmel", it read. "Gopal, there's good news for your town," Larry said, as he pointed to the paper. "You'll need to tell everybody about your church," Larry continued as he walked to his car.

Larry drove down the highway. He thought about Gopal and how his enthusiasm for the faith was so different than that of the average American. Things had changed so much over the years. The problem today was not that nobody had heard of Y'shua, but that everybody in America thought they knew all about Him. And that was the final point he needed to make to Larry and Sarah.

They were waiting for him at Martha's hot dog stand.

"Hi, Larry!" they said to him in unison as he climbed out of his car.

"Hello, Pastors!" Larry responded. They were sitting very close together today, he noticed. Good!

"Alright, I've got one more set of instructions for you, and then I have to leave town for a long time, perhaps years."

"What?" The two pastors were shocked. Jerry continued, "But things are just beginning to pop at the churches! We need your advice!"

"No, you don't. Not beyond what I'm going to tell you today."

The young adults exchanged glances and waited for Larry to continue. "But I'm not going to talk to you until we order lunch."

The three of them place their orders with Martha and sat back down to wait for the food.

"Ok, today I want to talk to you about how you stay on track with your churches, "Larry began "Here's what you'll need to do.

"First of all, any church leader needs to develop certain self-disciplines. Those disciplines include reading several chapters of the Bible every day – there are some great guides to help you read through the Bible in a year online – get one!"

"Yes sir!" Sarah almost saluted.

"Another discipline which is very important is to take at least fifteen minutes a day – a half an hour to a full hour is better – to pray about your people, your church, and yourself and whatever comes to mind. But don't pray the way most people pray – Prayer isn't supposed to be a one-sided babbling of wants and needs to God. People learn that form of prayer from most pastoral prayers, which are intended to be intercessory prayers."

Sarah said, "The plan I've heard before is where you Praise, Repent, Access, and Yield - P.R.A.Y. – get it?"

"Yes, I've heard of that method. I consider that method is more advanced, but not the prayer method of a mature Christian. Consider it a method for intermediate Christians." Larry responded.

"What do you mean?" Jerry asked.

"When new Christians begin to pray, they are often very formal with their prayer, perhaps following the 'Our Father' style of the Lord's Prayer. Then, people begin learning that you can ask anything of God in a prayer, so they do. The PRAY acronym is a further step, leading us to Praise God, to Repent of our actions, to Access God's grace and make our requests, and to Yield to God's decision about those requests.

"Another version of this is the ACTS acronym: Adoration, Confession, Thanksgiving, and Supplication. But both methods are still essentially one-sided – us to God, and they are also focused upon our requests.

"But there is a difference between praying in front of a congregation and private prayer. A mature Christian leader should understand that private prayer was meant to be a constant two-way conversation. 'Pray continually.' You speak, and the Holy Spirit sends you a reply. A good prayer time is like holding a conversation with a wise father-figure."

"You mean like talking to you," Sarah said with a twinkle in her eye.

"I love you, too, Sarah," Larry answered with a smile.

Continuing with his talk, Larry said, "As you pray, speak as though someone is in the room with you, for God is in the room with you. Give God an opportunity to speak, for God will not interrupt you – God is so polite. Listen for that still, small voice that is on the edge of your mind and follow the advice given.

"That's tough for most people to follow, "Jerry said. "Isn't that sort of like the voice that some schizophrenics listen to?"

Larry focused upon Jerry. "Yes, to the outsider it seems the same, but the difference is that the Holy Spirit will never harm you, will never contradict the Bible, and will give you accurate advice. People with mental problems or those who are truly possessed by evil spirits will soon be harmed if they follow those voices.

"So, follow the Holy Spirit. When in doubt, talk to each other – you are both very godly people and the two of you together will not easily be led astray. But always be sure that you are following the Holy Spirit and not some other voice – especially the voice of your own natural desires."

"What other self-disciplines should we develop?" Sarah wanted to know.

"If we consider that our journey toward personal holiness is the development of virtues and character, and the dropping of bad habits, then perhaps the best self-discipline is to truly work on your own personal evangelism a couple of hours a week. Oh, you'll be spending time training people, preparing sermons, and conducting church business, but the best way to develop yourself as a Christian is to actively find a handful of people to personally lead to Christ, because you can't help but become more holy, knowledgeable, and wise if you are really trying to be the best evangelist you can be. People will insist that you walk the walk as well as talk the talk, and they will ask you all sorts of questions about God and Christ. They will force you to grow, so always be looking to lead people personally to Christ….and beyond that to holiness."

This really hit Sarah. "Wow! I guess evangelism puts everything we're supposed to do altogether, doesn't it? I mean, you have to know your Bible, you have to love Christ, you have to love other people to be good at evangelism – and other people will know when you are faking because everybody these days is always expecting to find fakes."

Larry agreed with her. "That's right. You have to be authentic to lead people to Christ, and so you'll work on listening to the Holy Spirit so the fruits of the Spirit can be developed in you.

"One other thing you'll need to do is to learn how to really preach well. Timothy Keller and Fred Craddock have the best books on the subject – find those books and read them!"

"Thanks, Larry. We'll get copies." Jerry assured him.

"One last thing. There is only one thing we do as pastors which is on the same level as baptizing a new Christian."

"What's that?" Sarah asked.

"Helping another person become a pastor or missionary or ministry leader. Be sure to encourage your leaders of all ages to consider full-time ministry. It begins in junior high with pointing kids to consider the ministry as a career, and it continues when you find people in their twenties, thirties, and forties who should change careers. You can even help people in their fifties and sixties become pastors."

"What, a 65-year old new pastor? They don't have much time left, do they?" Jerry looked at Larry, and in that moment, in Larry's eyes, Jerry looked so-o-o young.

Larry responded. "I've known many pastors who were still preaching regularly into their nineties. That means a 65-year old still has 25 years of productive ministry or more ahead of them. Don't discount the older, retired folks. They can even start new churches because they have the advantage of not needing a pastoral income."

Jerry asked, "How about Shirley McDonald? What do you think of her becoming a pastor? She sure can pray!"

Larry was quick to respond, "Shirley would make a great pastor, because Shirley knows how to talk with the Lord, she reads her Bible every day, and she has enough grounding that she can explain passages to other people. She'd do well!"

Sarah was excited. "Wow! I never thought about helping an old woman become a pastor. I always thought you'd need to become a pastor right out of college!"

"With God, all things are possible. Just put them in touch with your denominational people who certify new pastors. And help them see the purpose for the last third of their lives. Can you imagine the impact that would be made if you each helped ten of your people become pastors – especially if you each helped five leaders plant a new church each? That's how the church grew in the days of Peter and Paul. Thank you, Martha!" Larry took his hot dogs from Martha and they began to eat.

The two young pastors exchanged a knowing glance.

Sarah spoke up, "By the way, Larry, we wanted to let you know – we're getting married!"

A huge smile lit up Larry's face. "That's the best news I've heard in months! When's the wedding?"

And they settled in to talk like any set of good friends. After another 30 minutes, Larry gave his goodbyes, got into his car, and headed toward the Interstate, passing two men who were putting in a huge sign that read, "New Homes for Sale" in front of a huge cornfield on the edge of town. "Now I know why I've been here," he thought.

He turned west onto I-70.

"Where are we going, Spirit?" Larry asked aloud in his car.

"Just keep driving. I'll let you know when to stop," came the still, small Voice of the Spirit.

"Ok. You're in charge!" Larry answered, and turned on the radio, set to Christian music.

Discussion and Thought Questions

1) How much of the Bible have you sat down and read by yourself?

2) How do you pray?

3) Have you considered personal evangelism to be a virtue-producing discipline? How do you suppose this works?

4) Does your church have a process for identifying and encouraging people to become leaders? What is that process?

5) Have you personally considered becoming a pastor or a missionary? Tell your story. If not, then, why not?

Epilogue

As Larry headed west, Pastors Jerry and Sarah saw the headline in the paper about the new housing development as they left the hot dog stand and began to talk about what this would do for their churches. At the grocery store, Donna also saw the headline and realized the new homeowners would need Christian childcare, and began to daydream about how she could organize that...

And Shirley McDonald had just finished reading her Bible passages with her lunch, finishing up the last three chapters of Matthew.

As she bowed her head in prayer, it struck her that her prayer of a year ago had been granted. Her church had recovered, with over 80 people attending last Sunday, including that young family from India, the Patel family that had been coming the last month. Excitement filled the church, especially with the report that Bobby, Suzy and Robert's son, had "no signs of cancer" at his last checkup. But what really struck her this morning was the passage she had just read:

"Then Jesus came to them and said, 'All authority in heaven and on earth has been given to me. Therefore, go and make disciples of all nations, baptizing them in the name of the Father and of the Son and of the Holy Spirit, and teaching them to obey everything I have commanded you. And surely, I am with you always, to the very end of the age.'"

She prayed, "God, I do believe that you gave Jesus 'all authority in heaven and on earth.' So I will go and, with Your help, 'make disciples of all nations, baptizing them in the name of the Father and of the Son and of the Holy Spirit, and teaching them to obey everything Jesus commanded us.'

"Please lead me to be a pastor or a missionary, for I so want to serve You. And I know that Your Son will be with me to the very end of the age.

"Amen"

And once again, she had a vision, a vision of a small, white, clapboard church surrounded by green hills. People were just pouring into the church, there was standing room only, and she walked up front in her robe, with her white hair glistening in the light streaming through the stained glass windows, turned around and said to the congregation in a loud, strong, uplifting voice:

"Welcome to the house of the Lord!"

She woke up. And Shirley believed.

THE END

Made in United States
North Haven, CT
16 October 2023

42829126R00057